ONCE A BIKER

The new Hennessey and Yellich mystery

When a death-bed confession leads to the reopening of a murder case, it doesn't bode well that both victims were members of a bikers' gang twenty years ago. As Detective Chief Inspector Hennessey and his team try to investigate, it seems the vow of silence is as strong as ever and someone is determined to keep old secrets dead and buried...

Peter Turnbull titles available from
Severn House Large Print

Chelsea Smile
Fire Burn
False Knight
Sweet Humphrey
Chill Factor
The Dance Master
Treasure Trove

ONCE A BIKER

Peter Turnbull

Severn House Large Print
London & New York

This first large print edition published 2009
in Great Britain and the USA by
SEVERN HOUSE PUBLISHERS LTD of
9-15 High Street, Sutton, Surrey, SM1 1DF.
First world regular print edition published 2007 by
Severn House Publishers Ltd., London and New York.

British Library Cataloguing in Publication Data

Turnbull, Peter, 1950-
  Once a biker. -- (A Hennessey and Yellich mystery)
  1. Hennessey, George (Fictitious character)--Fiction.
  2. Yellich, Somerled (Fictitious character)--Fiction.
  3. Police--England--Yorkshire--Fiction. 4. Cold cases
  (Criminal investigation)--Fiction. 5. Gang members--
  Crimes against--Fiction. 6. Detective and mystery stories.
  7. Large type books.
  I. Title II. Series
  823.9'14-dc22

  ISBN-13: 978-0-7278-7808-3

Printed and bound in Great Britain by
MPG Books Ltd, Bodmin, Cornwall.

One

She had found the hospice had a wholly unexpected air of happiness about it. The peace of the institution she could under-stand, and indeed expected, as with the atmosphere of resignation, but the happi-ness of those awaiting death was something that came as a surprise. The slight smile on the peaceful face of a person whose life was drawing inexorably to its close was a revela-tion. Quite quickly she had come to see it as the way of things, the patients accepting death with dignity, some whilst relatively young, and them saying how it was better to be a good parent for a short time than a bad parent for a long time, and other positive affirmations.

There were, however, the exceptions, and it was the exceptions that formed her caseload. There was the man who had towards his end recovered memories of the car crash that he, and he alone out of five men, survived. He had never forgotten the crash itself, but many long-blanked details had surfaced, commensurate with the increase in the morphine dosage. Another man, again a survivor, was haunted by the screams of his brother who had died in the fire from which he had escaped, memories all the more terrible because he was the elder brother and he had suggested they pour paraffin on the fire which they had lit in their parent's garage. There was the woman who had given up her children for adoption and who lay in her bed, refusing to interact with the other patients, pining away her final days.

All she could do with such patients was to talk to them, offer her sympathetic ear and assist in some form of psychological closure before the end. These patients were the exceptions, and the minority. In most cases the attitude was one of quiet acceptance, a little like, she thought, of the condemned person bowing their head to assist the hangman to affix the noose.

That morning she had parked her car and run on clicking heels through a refreshing rainfall that the parched land desperately needed, pushed open the main door of the building and exchanged a cheery good morning with the receptionist as she signed the fire regulation register notifying that she was in the building. She walked to her office towards the rear of the building and sat at her desk. She glanced out of the window for some reason, which eluded her, because the view from her window was of a high brick wall some six feet away. She let the phone purr twice before answering it.

'Gillian Stoneman,' she said gently.

'Ward One, Staff Nurse Beatty,' the caller responded in a warm Yorkshire accent.

'Hello...' She smiled down the phone. She knew Hilda Beatty very well. She thought her to be like the cornerstone of the building. She had worked long and hard at St Peter's and was in her late fifties. When she retired a real gap would be created.

'I think we need your help, Gillian.'

'Oh?' Gillian Stoneman reached for her

pen and a referral form.

'Yes ... one of our patients had a bad night ... just reading his notes now, the night staff asked me to alert you.'

'Oh?' Gillian Stoneman repeated.

'Yes, a patient by the name of Wells ... Tony, short for Anthony Wells ... only forty-five, one of the younger ones ... not the youngest we've had, but youngish.'

'Yes ... what's his prognosis?'

'Not good ... anytime now.'

'I see. What happened in the night?'

'No physical pain but twisting and turning in the bed, moving his head rapidly from side to side, getting out of the bed and banging his head against the wall.'

'Guilt?' Gillian Stoneman offered, slipping off her heels.

'Seems so. We see it from time to time but it usually surfaces earlier than this. He's been with us for about four weeks, normally he's very placid ... but last night he seemed to have been a totally different character, so we'd like to refer him. He really does need someone to talk to...'

'Yes. Where is the cancer?'

'Lungs ... kidneys ... liver ... all over ... like

I said, he could go at any time but his mind is whirring. We don't like to see them in this state so close to the end.'

'Yes ... is he awake now?'

'Yes.'

'I'll be there directly.'

Gillian Stoneman walked silently on the flat-soled shoes she wore when in the building to Ward One's nursing station and met Hilda Beatty who then directed her to a visiting room.

'We told him you were coming,' Hilda Beatty spoke in a low tone, almost a whisper, 'and he walked there himself. That wasn't easy for him, it would have been a bit like you and me attempting Everest ... just ten feet from his bed to the room but that was a real achievement.'

Gillian Stoneman steeled herself. Cancer, she found, had a terrible smell and she doubted that she would ever get used to it. The ward staff did well to smother the smell as best they could with disinfectant, air freshener, fresh flowers and, especially on days like that day, open windows, but the odour could never fully be overcome. It was particularly powerful in the closed confines of a visiting room.

Anthony 'Tony' Wells revealed himself to be short, pale, shrunken and frail, clearly the classic 'shadow of his former self'. He glanced up at Gillian Stoneman with pale, sunken eyes. He wore pyjamas and a dressing gown. He forced a smile. 'I'm glad I have seen one last pretty woman before I die.'

Gillian Stoneman sat in the chair opposite him and smiled. The smell in the room was almost too strong for her.

'Mean it ... you're very pretty. The nurses in here are very good, but they're past their sell-by date. Always had an eye for the ladies, always thought I'd be a dirty old man ... have to settle for being a dirty middle-aged man. How old are you?'

'Well, this is supposed to be about you Tony ... but I'm thirty-two.'

'You're not married?'

Gillian Stoneman glanced at her left hand. 'Nope.' She smiled. 'Time yet.'

'Well, don't leave it too long ... that's where I went wrong. This would be easier to bear if I knew I had left my seed behind me.'

Gillian Stoneman shifted herself in the

chair. 'The ward staff said that you seemed distressed in the night.'

'Yes...' The man's humour seemed to leave him, suddenly he seemed to be struggling. 'Yes, my mother and father are still alive ... poor dears, it's not right when your children predecease you ... and I have a brother and a sister.'

'Yes...'

'They'll have a grave to visit. It was only in the night that I realized how important that is ... a grave to visit.'

'It helps bring closure to bereaved people. The funeral is also important ... probably more so ... a public gathering to recognize the passing of a loved one and a friend.'

'Yes ... never thought of it like that.' Anthony Wells glanced out of the window at the garden of the hospice, at a gardener hoeing the flowerbed. 'He'll still be alive tomorrow ... he'll come to work and weed and dig and whatever else it is that gardeners do. He'll not give me a thought nor anyone else in here ... be up the Rose and Crown for his Monday pint. Me ... I'll ... well ... I will or I won't, depending on whether this is all or whether there is an afterlife ... but what you said about the funeral ... you don't have a funeral for the dead, do you? You have a funeral for the bereaved, they are the ones that benefit from the funeral service, the person in the coffin is past caring.'

'You could say that.'

The dying man, who looked to Gillian Stoneman to be very small in the dressing gown, returned his attention to her. 'What about them that just disappear?'

'That's always a worry.'

'For the relatives?'

'For the relatives it's torture ... the not knowing ... that is terrible.'

'No funeral to attend? No grave to visit?' The man stiffened as if fighting something, then relaxed. 'That isn't good.'

'Few things are worse than having a family member disappear.'

The man took a sharp breath and stiffened. 'This is the end,' he said as he smiled. 'I can feel it.'

'I'll get someone.' Gillian Stoneman made to stand.

'No! No! It's called Foxfoot Wood.'

'Foxfoot Wood?'

'Yes ... near York ... that's where we put

him ... about twenty years ago.'

'Him?'

'Terry North.'

'Who put him there? You mean buried him?'

The man nodded. His eyes closed. 'Now his family can have peace ... peace ... they've waited long enough. Foxfoot Wood ... near here.' He shuddered and was still.

Gillian Stoneman remained seated and then slowly stood, silently. She left the visitor's room, ensuring the door was closed behind her and walked slowly and calmly to the nursing station.

Hilda Beatty smiled as she approached. 'How did it go?' she asked.

Gillian Stoneman did not return the smile. 'It went well ... I think he said what he wanted to say, but you'll need the concealment trolley.'

Reginald Webster walked briskly along the CID corridor and tapped reverently on the frame of the doorway. 'A moment of your time, please, sir.'

'Yes, Reginald,' George Hennessey smiled at him. 'What have you got?'

'I would normally go to Sergeant Yellich as he is the senior officer on duty, but he's wrapped up in that serious assault which has just happened ... left me holding the fort.'

'No matter.' Hennessey put his pen down, 'Somerled will understand you're not going behind his back, he can't be in two places at once. Please take a seat...' He indicated the vacant chair in front of his desk with an extended and open palm.

'Thank you, sir.' Webster slid nervously on to the nearest chair. 'Lady came to the enquiry desk, wanting to report a murder...'

'A murder?'

'Yes, sir. So I saw her, she's a counsellor in the hospice of St Peter's ... which unbelievably is on St Peter's Close ... not sure that's intentional humour, sir.'

Hennessey grinned. 'Well, you know it's going back some years now ... many years, but my late wife once had an elderly relative whose life ebbed away in an old persons' home which proudly stood on a road called Terminal Way.'

Webster grinned; he appreciated the easing of the atmosphere. 'Well, dare say it

14

comes to us all, sir, and it came to a gentleman in St Peter's just this morning, but before he died, he made what appears to amount to a deathbed confession to the counsellor, a Miss Stoneman.'

'Interesting.'

'Yes, sir, I thought so too ... not the sort of confession to be dismissed.'

'No ... not at all.'

'The gentleman who died –' Webster consulted his notes – 'one Anthony Wells, named the deceased as one Terry North. Did the checks and a Terence North was reported as a missing person twenty-three years ago when he was twenty-five years of age. That fits with what Tony Wells told Ms Stoneman ... he said about twenty years ago ... and the deceased...'

'Wells?'

'Yes, sir.'

'He wasn't old to be in a hospice ... forty-five ... so that would make him of the same generation as Terry North.'

George Hennessey sat forward and rested his elbows on his desktop. 'Now, that is interesting.' He looked at Webster's youthful face, thin, angular. This was his first post in

15

plain clothes, a new boy, new to CID, new to Micklegate Bar, having spent his uniformed years in Wetherby. He had so far seemed keen, eager to please, eager to make a good impression. The enthusiasm, the interest was clearly there; only his endurance remained an unknown value. 'What do we know about Terry North?'

'Nothing, sir, no record at all. His occupation is given as self-employed.' Webster handed Hennessey the missing persons file. Hennessey read a local address, saw the photograph of an ordinary looking young man. The next of kin were given as his parents of the same address.

'And Wells? What do we know of him?'

'Oh...' Webster looked uncomfortable. 'Haven't checked yet, sir, just wanted to bring this to you as soon as...'

'Alright, but after twenty years, there's no urgency ... bring the senior CID officer as full a package as you can.'

'Yes, sir.'

Hennessey reached for his phone and jabbed a four-figure internal number. 'Did she say if Wells said where North was murdered?' He held the phone to his ear.

'Yes ... well ... if not murdered there, he was buried at a location called Foxfoot –' he glanced at his notes – 'yes, Foxfoot Wood ... given as being "near York" ... and no, again ... I'm sorry.'

Hennessey held up his hand. 'Alright, don't worry. Like I said, twenty years on, it's hardly a hot case ... this is definitely a very cold case ... but remember, the fullest possible package.'

'I'll find the location, sir,' Webster said and nodded.

'Good man. Ah, collator ... good, DCI Hennessey here ... any information about an Anthony Wells? Local gentleman, aged forty-five ... sorry, nothing else but there cannot be many Anthony Wells' in York of that age.' Hennessey grinned. 'No ... all information to DC Webster.'

Webster mouthed, 'Thank you, sir.'

'Alright, thank you.' Hennessey replaced the phone gently. 'Nothing to thank me for, Reg, detective constables are not put in charge of murder cases...'

'Understood, sir.'

'This case is yours, do you have a file number for it?'

17

'Again, not yet, sir. Just a series of interview notes and a twenty-year-old mis per file at the moment.'

'OK.' Hennessey handed Webster the missing person file on Terry North. 'That's the first thing to do, start a new file ... get a number from the collator. See what we know about Mr Wells deceased ... find Foxfoot Wood, by whatever means, then get the sniffer dogs there.' Hennessey paused and glanced out of his office window at tourists in multi-coloured clothing thronging the walls. He thought that they must be baking in the heat, it being sufficiently hot that the walls were shimmering. He turned to Webster. 'This will be your case until a body is found...'

'Yes, sir.'

'The sniffer dogs will either find human remains or they won't. If they don't, close the case ... it's all we can do. If they do ... if they do ... then I will become the interested officer with Sergeant Yellich as my number two.'

'Understood, sir.'

'You and Ventnor will be the foot soldiers.'

'Yes, sir.'

'Nothing like plunging in at the deep end, Reg.' Hennessey smiled. 'I'm all for shoving new boys in at the deep end ... you either sink or swim. OK, you've got work to do.'

Webster stood. 'Yes, sir. The lady who brought the information to us, she's still in the interview room ... you don't need to see her?'

'No, so long as we have her details, she's free to go with our gratitude.'

Hennessey emerged from the suffocating heat within the inflatable tent and felt grateful that the day was beginning to cool. Two hours earlier he thought, and breathing would not have been possible inside the plastic dome. 'Did you find it easily?' he asked of Webster.

'Yes, no problem, the dog found it within a matter of minutes of being unleashed.' He turned and smiled at a muscular springer spaniel, which by then was enjoying the shade and seeming to sense, with some satisfaction, that his duty was done.

'No ... sorry.' Hennessey smiled. 'I meant the wood, Foxfoot Wood. Confess I didn't know it was here ... so close to the city too.'

'Ah ... that was a little more difficult, sir.' Webster brushed a fly from his face. 'I glanced at the Ordnance Survey map of the area ... combed it, no luck...'

'Really, a wood this size?' Hennessey glanced round him, there was a solid stand of trees which filled the hundred-and-fifty-yard distance from the clearing to the road where the police vehicles were parked and it seemed to him that the wood extended for many hundreds of yards in every direction from the clearing.

'Oh, it's clearly marked, sir ... by its official name, Five Acre Wood.'

'Ah...'

'Tried the Internet even ... no result ... phoned estate agents who seemed to specialize in rural properties...'

'That was good thinking.'

'Sir ... eventually I went up to the canteen at lunch time and just asked for everybody's attention and an experienced constable said he believed the name to be an alternative name for Five Acre Wood ... and here we are...'

'And here we are.' Hennessey glanced around him. The inflatable tent, the uniformed police officers in short-sleeved white shirts, the SOCO officers with cameras, standing together, being not fully accepted by the police officers, the dog and its handler. 'And here we are,' he repeated. 'Still, you did well to find the body so rapidly in a wood as dense as this and as large as this.'

'Oh, we have PC King, the dog handler, to thank for that, sir.'

'Really?' Hennessey responded with alertness as his eye was caught by the movement of a slender, short-haired woman, carrying a highly polished Gladstone bag, weaving confidently between the trees as she approached the clearing. He turned to the nearest uniformed officer and asked him to carry Dr D'Acre's bag. The constable responded promptly and ran to meet the woman. 'Really?' Hennessey said again.

'Yes, I explained the situation to him and he looked about him and he said, "Well, nobody's going to bury anything in these trees, you'll never penetrate the root plates" and he meshed his fingers together like so ... "What we need is a clearing", he said.' Webster separated his hands. '"and then we'll slip Hector ... ", that's the dog...'

'I gathered.'

'So we probed the wood and one of the constables ... I have his name in my book for the report...'

'Yes?'

'He came across this clearing and alerted us. PC King slipped Hector, who started to criss-cross the clearing ... and within a minute, he started to paw at a specific location and PC King said, "I'd dig there, if I were you".'

'So you dug.' Hennessey began to like Webster, he was a man who clearly believed credit should be given where it is due. He was even going to give credit to the constable who stumbled on the clearing. A lesser man would not have done so, and an even lesser man, in George Hennessey's view, would have attempted to take it for himself. Webster was going to be an asset. 'And you found what you found just two feet down?'

'Yes, sir ... human remains. Could just as easily have been someone's pet dog ... we've done that before, but we got a strike at the first dig. So it is your case now, sir.'

'For my sins.'

'I'll write my report up to the point that we contacted yourself, SOCO and the forensic pathologist.'

'Who is here now.' Hennessey looked beyond Reginald Webster, who turned in response.

'Good afternoon, ma'am.' Hennessey smiled warmly.

'Ma'am,' said a surprised Webster who was clearly expecting the forensic pathologist to be male.

'Gentlemen.' Dr D'Acre had a warm, soft, educated voice. 'In the tent, I presume?'

'Yes, ma'am, skeletal remains ... no need for the police surgeon to pronounce life extinct.'

'Indeed, straight to me.' Dr D'Acre smiled; she wore no make-up save a trace of lipstick and was dressed in a sober light-weight dress, which was belted around her middle.

'Please escort the doctor to the tent, Mr Webster,' Hennessey asked, a trifle annoyed that he had to do so. He thought Webster might be a little short on initiative but that could be addressed. He was still certain that the man was going to be an asset to the team.

Webster led Dr D'Acre to the tent, followed by the constable who carried her bag. Moments later Webster and the constable emerged and shortly afterwards, were followed by Dr D'Acre, carrying her bag.

'Adult male. Not been down there very long, so it will be of interest to you. I can still detect flesh and clothing.'

'We think twenty years, ma'am.' Hennessey blinked in the sunlight.

'That would be about my guess. I'll take a soil sample, that will help determine the length of time he has been down there, but that's all I can do here. The body can be removed if you have taken all the photographs you have to take.'

Hennessey glanced at Webster.

'All done, sir ... all done before you arrived. I asked the Scene of Crime Officer to remain in case we find anything beneath the body.'

Hennessey smiled at him.

'Well, I'll go on ahead.' Dr D'Acre glanced at Hennessey. 'Will you be observing the post-mortem for the police, Chief Inspector?'

'Yes ... I will.'

Dr D'Acre walked back towards the road, the same constable walking behind her, carrying her bag.

'I'll supervise the retrieval of the body, Reg.'

'Yes, sir.'

'Then I'll leave you with the location. As you suggest, see if there's anything beneath the body or around the body.'

'Yes, sir. We'll also sift the soil that covered the body ... a lot of it came up in large chunks, as you see, because of the dry weather. They could contain gold dust.'

Hennessey nodded. Lately it had been DS Yellich who had been more on the ball than he had been and now it was this young man, younger than his own son, who was thinking of things he should have thought of. His pension was calling his name more and more loudly with each day that passed.

George Hennessey stood against the wall wearing green disposable coveralls. His purpose was to observe, and he could only approach the stainless steel table if invited.

The skeletal remains of the deceased, believed to be one Terence 'Terry' North, lay on the furthest right of the four tables in the pathology laboratory.

Dr D'Acre stood by the corpse, studying it carefully, and was dressed, as Hennessey, in green disposable coveralls which also encased her feet and her head, consisting of five items of clothing, a hat, a vest, leggings and a pair of slippers. Eric Filey, the pathology laboratory assistant, was also similarly dressed and stood back from the table holding a 35mm camera with a flash attachment. Above the table, as indeed above all four tables, was a microphone attached to an anglepoise arm, which was affixed to the ceiling. The room itself was illuminated by filament bulbs, the glare of which was contained by sheets of opaque perspex, and smelled strongly of formaldehyde.

'We recovered some artefacts that might be of interest to you, Chief Inspector,' Dr D'Acre said as she turned to Hennessey. 'And some remnants of clothing which we have bagged and will send to Wetherby for analysis.'

'Clothing?' Hennessey could not conceal

his surprise. 'After twenty years?'

'Oh ... it's not unusual. The soils in the Vale of York are damp, as you know, the rainfall we have, the flooding in the Spring after the thaw ... but despite that recognizable clothing was recovered ... leather in the main ... remnants of a padded jacket, padded trousers and heavy, heavy boots.'

'A biker?'

'Yes, that's what Eric and I thought. In fact it's an inescapable conclusion ... but sans helmet, which is significant because he appears to have been slain by a blow to the head. Can we have a photograph of this please, Eric?' Dr D'Acre stepped back and to one side, allowing the portly Eric Filey to manoeuvre himself into the optimum position to take a photograph of the skull where Dr D'Acre indicated.

'A blow to the head?' Hennessey lowered his head and shut his eyes against the flash.

'A concentrated blow rather than a linear fracture ... the sort of injury that would be caused by being attacked by a hammer, rather than an iron bar. The fractures radiate from a central point.'

'Yes...' Hennessey opened his eyes after he

27

heard the camera click and had seen the flash through lowered eyelids. 'I have seen that injury before.'

'Many times, I imagine.' Dr D'Acre allowed herself an uncharacteristic smile.

'Too many times, ma'am.'

'We have other injuries, other fractures ... ribs ... here, and here ... Photographs, please, Eric, see ... here ... here ... and just here.' Again Dr D'Acre stepped backwards to allow the laboratory assistant access to the corpse, the arms, the clavicle ... both clavicles. 'That would have disabled him –' she turned to Hennessey – 'both clavicles...'

'The collar bones?'

'Yes, both have been fractured.'

Hennessey noticed Eric Filey raise the camera with purposefulness and again closed his eyes.

'That would have prevented him from moving his arms ... his arms would have been immobilized,' Dr D'Acre explained.

'Interesting.' Again Hennessey saw the flash and opened his eyes.

'The femur...' Dr D'Acre once again examined the skeleton. 'He has fractures all over him. I will have his body X-rayed and then I can count all the fractures but I can say now that he sustained a very serious assault ... blows were rained on him from every angle and once the clavicles were fractured, he could not defend himself. The ankles have been fractured ... he would not have been able to escape. He annoyed somebody...'

'It seems so.'

'This is as serious a sustained assault as I have come across. I would think the blow to the head would be the coup de grâce. There is no other injury to the head or face that I can detect ... so he was conscious when the blows were raining down on his body, there is little point in battering somebody like that if they were life extinct...'

'I'll say. So he knew he was being attacked ... he was conscious?'

'I would think ... this seems to be retribution being exacted.'

'Are the fractures the same age as the head injury?'

'A good question and I would say they are indeed *perimortem* ... no old healed fractures and so many of them that they are almost certain to be contemporary with each other.' She paused. 'This young man suffered dreadfully before he died ... and probably knew he was going to be killed. Somebody wanted more than death for him, he was given a dreadful hiding for some infraction and then despatched.'

'More than one attacker, ma'am?'

'Hard to tell, once his legs had been disabled by fracturing the ankles and once the arms had been disabled by fracturing the collar bones ... then ... yes ... then one person could have occasioned all those injuries, but I tend to think not. I feel in my waters that this person, this young man, was attacked by a mob.'

'Well, your waters have proved right before, ma'am. I can go along with that...'

'Thank you ... your faith means much.' She paused. 'I understand that you have an idea of his identity, one Terence North?'

'Yes, ma'am.'

'Well, in that case, I will send a tissue sample to Wetherby, they can extract the DNA profile. He seems to have been a young man when he died.'

'About twenty-five years of age, we understand.'

'Yes ... that would concur with my obser-
vation ... and in the ground for the last
twenty years ... so he'd be mid-forties now
had he lived ... He will have living relatives
... probably even one or both parents. If you
can't get a DNA match because he has no
living relatives or he is not Terence North,
then we'll go on to the next stage ... facial
reconstruction and all the rest of it, but I
don't want to do that if we can get a positive
match using the DNA. I am asked to
confine myself within a budget. You will
probably have read about the cutbacks ...
jobs are going to be axed in the Area Health
Authority ... won't affect me, fortunately,
but those more lowly than I in terms of their
position, the nursing auxiliaries ... the port-
ers ... they will be in fear of losing their jobs
... so it's not a time of bounty and plenty.
Received a memo yesterday asking me to
avoid unnecessary expenditure. So I'll wait
until the DNA matches, if it does it's the
end of the story, he is Terence North and
he was most cruelly battered to death by
person or persons unknown.'
'Thank you.'
'I will trawl for poisons, of course, that is a

31

simple and inexpensive procedure but it does cover a base. These injuries could be post-mortem ... but their extent ... I doubt it, frankly.'

'I doubt it too, ma'am.' Hennessey turned to go.

'No injuries to the face...' Dr D'Acre said suddenly.

'Sorry?'

'No facial injuries.'

'Suggesting ... ma'am?'

'Well I am not a forensic psychologist, fascinating field that it is ... and I do hate to encroach...'

'Oh, encroach all you like, ma'am, all help gratefully received.'

Dr D'Acre smiled. 'Well, it's possibly old hat and discredited now but I did once read that people attacked with passion, that is with hatred, are attacked on their face ... the face is the focus of the hostility and anger...'

'Yes, I have also read that.'

'Well ... no personally felt emotion here ... no damage to the face, a very dispassionate execution, but somebody wanted to hurt him before they killed him. Interesting.'

'Very. Oh, and you mentioned some items

taken from the body?' Hennessey asked.

'Oh, yes ... Eric...'

Eric Filey laid the camera down on the bench that ran along the opposite wall of the pathology laboratory and picked up a productions bag and with alert reverence walked silently across the industrial grade linoleum that covered the floor and handed it to Hennessey. Hennessey took the bag and bowed his head and spoke words of thanks.

He took his leave of Dr D'Acre and Eric Filey and went to the male changing rooms and peeled off the coveralls, which he folded casually and deposited them in a yellow 'sin bin'. He felt hot and clammy and ached for a shower ... the drip of water from a faulty washer in the showers was, he found, enticing and difficult to resist, but he had no towel. Then, remembering school days and basic training in the Royal Navy when he found not having a towel was unacceptable as an excuse for not having a shower, he removed the remainder of his clothing and stood rejoicing as the lukewarm spray of crystal clear water cooled and refreshed him.

Later he sat on the bench in the changing room and examined the items handed to him by Eric Filey as the sun, streaming through the windows, dried his flesh. A zip fastener that could have come from anywhere, what seemed to be the remains of a ballpoint pen ... a belt buckle with no distinguishing features or marks ... coins ... low value and none less than twenty years old by their dates. He smiled as he thought what a spanner in the works would have been caused by a coin of, say, five years' vintage. His interest was aroused by one item, a dull clasp of the type worn by women in their hair ... appeared to be bronze but the decorative work was so elaborate and fine in its detail that the artefact was, Hennessey felt, most certain to be made of gold. It may be an additional aid to identification of the deceased, should one be needed.

Walking down the corridor, refreshed and relaxed after the shower, he glanced at Dr D'Acre's office door as he passed and read the plate: Louise D'Acre MD (Leeds) MRCP, DMJ (Path). A clever, clever lady, he mused, and thought of the interior of the office, cramped, with photographs of a horse and three pre-teen and teenage children framed proudly on the walls. He pondered knocking on the door but walked on, knowing that such an intrusion would not be welcome or appreciated.

He left the medium rise slab-sided building that was York District Hospital and, feeling refreshed after the shower, was grateful that the heat of the day had largely subsided. The sun was by then still visible in the north-west but was casting noticeably longer shadows. He strolled at a leisurely pace down Clarence Street and then the narrower Gilleygate. He entered the graceful curve of St Leonard's as the art gallery was closing for the day. Many tourists walked the pavements, though not as many as earlier in the day and they seemed, to Hennessey, to be walking at a slower, gentler pace. The eagerness of exploring the ancient city had left them as the day progressed and now they seemed to saunter, more interested in looking for a good restaurant than in museums and medieval buildings.

Hennessey joined the walls at Lendal Bridge because, as every resident in the city knows, the most rapid way to transit the city is by walking the walls, and also because, he reasoned, that being fifteen or twenty feet above the road, the walls would be cooler. He knew the first would be true and was delighted that the second was also true. He was not a hothouse plant, finding heat uncomfortable, and would be happier to spend two weeks in Aberdeen in January than he would be to spend two weeks in Crete in July. Perverse thinking in the eyes of bronzed sun-seekers perhaps, but he had never been a sun-seeker.

He glanced to his left as he walked, at the new buildings within the walls, and was again sorrowed and angered that the original station with its curved platform and serrated roofline had been allowed to be demolished to make way for a soulless office block. The old station building had been there one day and gone the next, which had saddened and surprised Hennessey, believing it to have been a listed building. To his right was the present-day station with its roof which, when built in the nineteenth century, was claimed to be the largest unsupported roof in the world. He left the walls at Micklegate Bar and stepped into Micklegate, and as he did so he glanced up at the gate itself, an arched stone structure through which modern day traffic passes in alternating single file, being strictly controlled by traffic lights. It is probably the most interesting of the gates of the city, Hennessey pondered. Being on the road to and from London meant that every monarch from the Conqueror until the twentieth century, when visiting kings and queens began to arrive by rail or air, had passed beneath its arch. And the spikes too, where heads of traitors were impaled, gruesome and clearly visible, the last head being impaled as late as 1745. Hennessey turned his eyes downward from the spikes, checked the traffic lights, and crossed the road into Micklegate Bar police station as the road traffic was halted to allow foot passengers to cross.

He acknowledged the reverential 'sir' of the constable at the enquiry desk, opened the door marked 'staff only', and checked his pigeonhole in the nest of holes, which stood just inside the doorway. There was, he saw, nothing of urgent consequence. He walked on down the CID corridor and passed the office shared by Thompson Ventnor and Reginald Webster. Webster was at his desk, writing.

'Working late?' Hennessey stood in the doorway; he spoke softly, warmly.

'Just finished now, sir.' Webster looked up, alert, confident. 'Completing my recording on the finding of the body of Terry North ... if it is he. I'll be doing the visits you requested tomorrow, sir.'

'Good. Take DC Ventnor with you.'

'Yes, sir, the foot soldiers ... I remember.'

'All cogs in the same machine, Reginald. We all do our bit ... the largest machine can fail if the humblest component doesn't do its job.'

'Understood, sir.'

'Anything in the grave? I mean anything else?'

'Well yes, sir.' Webster reached for a cellophane production bag which stood on the corner of his desk. 'We found these.' He handed the bag to Hennessey.

'Car keys.' Hennessey looked in the bag.

'Probably motorcycle keys,' Webster offered. 'One of the uniforms is a keen motorcyclist, he found them and identified them as bike keys.'

'Would fit with the protective leather clothing and the boots.'

'That's what I thought too.' Webster arched his back and flexed his shoulders as he momentarily turned from Hennessey and glanced out of his office window. Ventnor and he had a very good view of the staff car park and the glistening mixture of old and new, angular and curved buildings beyond. 'What do you make of the wallet, sir?'

'I was looking at it. Have you opened it?'

'No fear, sir, it crumbled to the touch ... don't know what evidence we'll destroy by opening it ... off to Wetherby for you, me thought.'

'Good man, you thought correctly, the wallet will have to be scientifically examined ... one for the lab boys. We'll send it tomorrow.'

'Is the ID confirmed, sir?'

'Not yet. When you visit the North family tomorrow, if they are still there and alive – a lot can happen in twenty years – ask them for a DNA sample. I mean, ask them if they will provide one, one of our forensic scientists can visit them at home. I'm sure they'll oblige.'

Gillian Stoneman was unable to sleep because of the heat, she lay naked under a thin sheet listening to the sound of the night, an owl, the clicking of heels of a lone female foot passenger walking on the pavement below her window, the occasional car horn, the whirring of the diesel engine of the buses on the main road a few hundred yards distant and the solid and secure sound of an express train as it travelled north or south, picking up speed after its stop at York, for she knew that no train ever goes through York without stopping.

She loved her job, pay was dreadful, but valued the depth, enabling people to come to terms with their end, helping them lay demons of long held guilt or terrible experience. She met the cruelty of life in the cases of young men and women succumbing to an elderly person's illness, and she witnessed the quiet courage and dignity of those about to die. That day she had met something she had never before encountered, the fearsome self-obsession of a man who could not, had not, realized the importance of a grave to the bereaved until just hours before his own passing.

Terrifying.

It was Monday, the seventeenth of June, 23.42 hours.

Two

Tuesday, 18 June, 09.05 hours – 11.32 hours
in which leads are followed.

Thompson Ventnor and Reginald Webster drove the short distance from Micklegate Bar police station to Tang Hall. Tang Hall, low rise, densely packed council accommodation, where motorcycles are chained to lampposts, where neighbourly disputes are settled in the street. Quite neat in terms of its appearance but hostile, stressed, violent behind the clipped privet hedgerows. This is part of the Famous and Faire that the tourists do not see.

Ventnor drove to the last known address of Terence North, on Flaxman Mount, deep inside the estate, where the hedgerows are not as neatly clipped as on the main roads or the roads on the edge of the estate, where the paint isn't as fresh and roads and pavements are more pitted. He parked the car opposite number eight and he and Webster walked up the path, opened the door into the block and walked up the stairs to the second floor. The walls of the stairway were covered in graffiti, and the plaster was chipped extensively.

The two officers stood side by side as Webster tapped the door, using the classic police officer's knock, tap, tap ... tap. The door was opened hurriedly by a man who appeared to be in his early seventies. He was thin, gaunt, yet had clearly dressed to greet his visitors, a clean yellow short-sleeved shirt, white slacks, polished shoes. His hair had been dampened and neatly combed with a parting on his left-hand side.

'Mr North?' Webster showed his ID.

'Yes, sir.'

'I am DC Webster, this is DC Ventnor ... we spoke on the phone.'

'Yes, sir ... about our Terry?'

'Yes.'

The man stepped aside. 'Please come in, gentlemen.'

Ventnor and Webster stepped into the cool

interior of the hallway. The house smelled strongly of air freshener and furniture polish, as if, following Webster's phone call of thirty minutes earlier announcing their intention to visit, 'with some information about Terence', the Norths had hurriedly done what they could to clean their home in order to receive their visitors.

'Just here, Mr North?' Ventnor indicated a room at the end of the corridor, to the right.

'Yes, sir ... just go in.'

Ventnor and Webster entered the room, where an elderly lady sat by the fireplace in an upright chair, the sort that Ventnor recognized as having a spring loaded seat so as to assist the occupant in rising. A walking frame stood in front of the chair.

'You'll have to excuse Edith,' the man said with a genuinely apologetic tone, 'she can't stand well these days.'

'Please ... no matter.' Webster smiled at Mrs North who raised a bony misshapen hand in acknowledgement. Her hair seemed to both Ventnor and Webster to have been freshly brushed. It was obvious then to the officers that the house cleaning and tidying had all been done by the elderly Mr North and when he had done that, he had combed his wife's hair and then changed into fresh clothing and combed his own hair. It seemed to both Ventnor and Webster to represent a lot of work, a lot of energy expended, by an elderly man. They were touched by his humility.

'Please, gentlemen, do take a seat.' Mr North indicated the settee, an inexpensive PVC covered item, and Webster and Ventnor sat on it, side by side, while North took his chair on the opposite side of the fireplace from his lady wife.

'Well,' Webster initiated the conversation, 'as I said on the phone, we might have some information about Terence.'

'Is he well?' Edith North had a strong voice. 'He was always a good boy ... I knew he'd come back one day.'

Ventnor winced inwardly, Webster looked at the carpet. Mr North sat back resignedly in his chair as if he knew that the officers had come with bad tidings, that all the effort that had gone into cleaning the house and combing their hair had not been to welcome good news but bad. Eventually the silence that greeted Edith North's response reached her and she began to make a strange, high-pitched wailing sound.

'Did ... I mean,' Webster struggled, 'when Terence disappeared did he own a motorcycle?'

'Yes ... his machine. We didn't like it but what can you tell a young man?'

'Oh, Claude...' Edith North appealed to her husband.

'Alright, Edith, just wait, see what the gentlemen have to tell us.'

'Well, there just is no easy way to tell you this,' Webster spoke, 'so I'll just say it. We have found a body ... a body has been found in a shallow grave ... it is male ... there are indications of the person having been dressed in motorcyclist's clothing, leather jacket, trousers and heavy boots...'

'Yes, sir.' Claude North sat back in his chair and seemed to let his eyes wander out of the window. Webster followed his gaze and saw the flat roofs of the houses on the opposite side of Flaxman Mount, with a clear, cloudless blue sky beyond. 'After this length of time ... I know I never said anything, Edith, but I knew...'

'I always thought...' Edith North's voice

faltered. She did not complete the sentence.

'I have to tell you that identification is not yet certain, which is why we have called. There are a number of ways we can identify the body but the simplest would be to do a DNA check.'

'DNA?'

'Deoxyribonucleic acid,' Webster spoke softly. 'Apparently we all have a unique DNA signature, but blood relatives have similar signatures.'

'I have heard of that on the television,' Claude North said and nodded. 'I have heard of that.'

'Well, if our forensic scientist can call on you and take a swab from both yours and Mrs North's mouth, that would indicate if you were the parents of the young man whose body was found. It's called a buccal swab and in itself it isn't conclusive, but it will show us quickly if you are not the parents; however, if it indicates that you may be, our scientist would then have to take a blood sample ... just a pinprick, to do a deeper analysis which would prove that you are his parents, and if so, then ... well...'

'Well, then it is our Terry.'

'I'm afraid so ... yes...'

'Well, certainly we'll help but won't a strand or two of his hair do? I mean I only know what I've seen on television.' He nodded to the screen in the corner of the room beside Edith North's chair. He clearly had a relaxed view of the television whilst his wife, despite her failing health, was obliged to watch it from a more acute angle – not uncomfortably so but the easy viewing was his.

'His hair?'

'Yes...' Claude North looked at Webster. 'We kept his room just as it was on the day he left, nothing has been touched, no one else has slept in his bed.'

'We don't get visitors, you see,' Edith North explained. 'No one ever comes to see us.'

'But we don't mind,' Claude North continued, 'there's just us ... we're happy enough.'

'Terence was your only child?'

'Aye ... just the one. It was difficult for our Edith ... Terry's arrival.'

'He didn't want to put me through that again, so we never had another,' Edith North added. 'Just the three of us.'

'I see ... well, yes, a hair sample of his would be excellent.'

'This way, gents.' Claude North stood. He led the two officers into a room which was first on the left as one entered the flat and which revealed itself to be a bedroom of modest proportions. It was neatly kept. 'Our Edith changed the sheets once or twice over the years,' he explained as he walked towards a chest of drawers, 'but apart from that, it's the same as the day that Terry left.' He took a man's hairbrush which had a comb embedded in the bristles and handed it to Webster, being the nearest officer. 'Plenty of Terry's hair on that,' he observed. 'That's all his stuff ... better than taking one of them swabs...'

'Indeed.' Webster took the hairbrush, holding it delicately between two fingers, and dropped it into a self-sealing cellophane sachet. 'We'll get this off to Wetherby by urgent despatch.'

'Wetherby, sir?'

'Yes ... jolly old Wetherby ... that's where the Home Office forensic science laboratory is situated.'

'I see, sir.'

'So we'll get that off today, by courier.'

'Courier?'

'Motorcycle courier.'

'I see ... sir, how did you link our Terry to the body which was found? Was there a name or something?'

'No ... no name.' Then Webster told him how it was that the police were first alerted to the unmarked and shallow grave.

'Tony Wells?' Claude North shook his head. 'That's a name I have never heard. Knew a Wells once, years ago ... but that was Charlie Wells and he died soon after I met him ... but Tony? Let's go and see if our Edith knows.'

'Wasn't that one of his mates?' Edith North offered when the three men had once again rejoined her in the home's tidy sitting room.

'Was it? I never heard of him.'

'Well, I'm sure I have. Terry used to run with a wild pack of wolves, he got into trouble with the law...'

'Yes, we know ... criminal damage, causing affray, drunk and disorderly conduct, usual biker stuff, but even then that was the mild end – we've known bikers do an awful lot worse than that.'

'He was a good lad really.' Claude North walked to the window, placed his hands on the windowsill and stared down into Flaxman Mount. 'Just got in with a bad lot. He would have settled, got married and we'd be grandparents now.'

'Maybe even great grandparents.' Edith North stared blankly into space. 'So he's not coming home after all? Oh ... my Terry ... who'd do that to him?'

'Well, that is what we are here for,' Ventnor spoke solemnly. 'We might have prosecuted Terry in the past, but we are also here to see that his killer is brought to justice.'

'Thank you, sir.' Claude North turned from the window and faced the two detectives. 'Thank you.'

'Please keep his room just as it is. If the DNA from the brush and comb is a match with the DNA taken from the body, it will prove that the body is Terry's. If that is the case, we'd like to search his room.'

'Of course.'

'And we can bury him.' Edith North spoke more to herself than to her husband. 'Then at least we know where he is.'

'We are deeply sorry to have to call on you at a time like this,' Hennessey apologized. Beside him he could feel Somerled Yellich's discomfort. 'We could call later...'

'No...' Garry Wells spoke softly. He was a well-set man in his sixties; he stood in front of the fireplace.

'It's a relief.' His wife, who also stood, looked out of the window as she spoke. She was taller than her husband, a slender body and Hennessey was able to see the young woman in her, quite a beauty he thought. 'Now he's gone, it's a relief.'

'If he had to go young, it's better this way –' Garry Wells looked at his wife – 'natural causes ... no one to blame. At least he survived his danger years ... those motorcyclists.'

'Ugh,' Juliette Wells shuddered.

'Well, it's about that time we'd like to talk to you ... if we can pick your brains? It's not about Anthony as such.'

'Well, that's a relief ... please take a seat.'

Hennessey and Yellich had consulted the voter's roll and had found that Garry and Juliette Wells still occupied the same address that was given as Anthony Wells' home address when at the age of seventeen he had his first recorded conviction for criminal damage. There was, they reasoned, little purpose in going to the flat where he was believed to have lived alone. The family address was given as Chantry Crescent, Bishopthorpe. They drove there, with Yellich at the wheel. The Wells' house revealed itself to be a solid 1930s semi-detached house with a neatly kept garden and clematis growing up a lattice support attached to the house. A new, but modest motorcar stood gleaming on the drive. Hennessey and Yellich left the car with the windows partially wound down so as to let the interior breathe in the heat and walked to the front door. Yellich pressed the bell, which made a continuous ring. The door had been opened promptly, the two officers, having identified themselves, were invited into the house, which appeared neatly kept with the air solid with the fragrance of furniture polish. They were shown into the living room at which point Hennessey apologized for calling 'at a time like this'.

'It's really about Tony's biker days,' Hennessey explained, once he and Yellich and also the Wells were seated.

'He never recovered,' Garry Wells said. 'Those bikers ... his life was hardly begun when they corrupted him. He just never did anything, not like our Dennis.'

'Dennis?'

'Our other lad.' Wells pointed to the mantelpiece on which stood a framed photograph of a soldier in dress uniform. 'Twenty-three years' service with the Royal Engineers. He's a sergeant major, leaving soon with a good pension and plenty of working life left in him. Married, two children ... but Anthony ... he just didn't do anything. Long-term unemployed, in the main. Except get into trouble with the police.'

'Yes.' Hennessey nodded. 'Detective Sergeant Yellich and I glanced at his record before we came here but he has not been convicted of any offence for a few years; he was a responsible member of the public.'

'Well, thank you for saying that but ... well ... he was a very selfish person. He wanted everything and he wanted it yesterday. He was our son, he died young in life of a cruel illness, but he was no saint. But your kind words are welcome, sir. Thank you.'

Hennessey inclined his head. 'He did some good...'

'He did?'

'Yes ... there's no reason why you should not know. One of the last things ... in fact the very last thing he did was to disclose the whereabouts of a dead body.'

'He did what!' Garry Wells face flushed purple. 'You mean he was involved in a murder! And that's a good thing?'

'We thought it was nothing more than laddish behaviour,' Juliette Wells appealed, 'now you are saying he was a murderer...'

'We are not saying anything of the kind, Mrs Wells, we are not saying that. Anthony may have had some knowledge, some first-hand knowledge ... He may have been told about it by some other person and perhaps kept quiet so as to observe some code of honour ... but yesterday he broke with that code. He broke his silence and told us where we'd find a body. He did that because he felt for the relatives of the deceased, he did that so that they might have closure ... it was a very unselfish act.'

'He redeemed himself,' Juliette Wells

snarled and was, thought Hennessey, unduly cynical. 'Well ... well ... well.'

'So who? There was nothing on the news about this.'

'We haven't issued a press release ... not yet ... we will when we have identified the person.'

'That's a bit unusual. I mean it seems that unidentified bodies are in the news from time to time.'

'Yes, that is the normal course of action because normally we have difficulty identifying the remains but in this case, we believe we know the identity of the body and so wanted to break the news to the relatives before we make the press release.'

'Who was it?'

'Can't tell you yet, two of my officers are with the family now getting evidence that will confirm the deceased's identity one way or the other.'

'Oh ... that DNA stuff you hear about?'

'Yes,' Hennessey said nodding, 'that DNA stuff.'

'Probably was one of that gang ... what did they call themselves?'

'The Dungeon Kings,' Juliette Wells replied and shook her head.

'Yes, the Dungeon Kings ... they took their name from the York dungeons ... you know, the tourist attraction. They just seemed to exist to get into fights with rival biker gangs.'

'And get drunk,' Juliette Wells sniffed. 'They did that a lot.'

'Well, it's really the gang, the Dungeon Kings, we are interested in.' Hennessey saw Yellich reach into his pocket for his notebook and ballpoint.

'We never did meet any of them ... would not allow them here and Anthony wouldn't bring them here ... he knew better.'

'He knew better alright,' Juliette Wells echoed. 'He knew a lot better than to bring them here.'

'Biker groups have their own pub,' Hennessey prompted. 'Which one did they use?'

'The Three Cranes, I think.'

'It was the Three Cranes, out by Stamford Bridge,' Garry Wells confirmed.

Hennessey and Yellich glanced at each other.

'Why, is that where the body was found?' Garry Wells leaned forward. 'I saw you glance at each other. Is that where he was buried?'

'Well ... not a million miles from there.'

'That's where they used to go. He'd go roaring off on his machine ... trailing his legs behind him.'

'You'll be sorting through his possessions, I assume.'

'Aye ... I assume we will, we'll leave it until after the funeral, though, and "we" won't be doing anything ... I will do it.'

'Oh, but he's my son,' Juliette Wells argued.

Garry Wells held up his hand and his wife stopped talking. 'If there's anything there that you shouldn't see ... you'd better not see it, so I'll be clearing his flat. Me ... just me.'

Juliette Wells did not argue again.

'Well, should you find anything relating to the Dungeon Kings, you'll let us know?'

'Yes, I will. I was in the fire service for many years – the fire service and the police are sister agencies – of course I'll let you know.'

'Much appreciated.' Hennessey and Yellich stood.

★   ★   ★

Driving away from Bishopthorpe, Yellich said, 'That'll be a great name for Jeremy ... the Three Cranes...'

'Oh?'

'Aye, we're teaching him car cricket, we learned about it at the support group. It's educational and teaches the children to be observant.'

'Really?' Hennessey glanced at him.

'Only really works when you're not on a motorway because you look for pub names, that's a rich culture in itself ... some pubs are hundreds of years old.'

'I know.'

'Well, the game is, every time you see a pub named after a living creature, including humans, you score a run for each leg the creature has.'

'I follow.'

'And when you see a pub which is named after something which has no legs, you lose a wicket.'

'So the Three Cranes would mean six runs.'

'That's it, boss, and it would teach Jeremy what a crane is and how they stand on one leg ... And a pub called the Hare and

Hounds would be twelve runs ... the hounds is plural so there must be at least two dogs ... so that's eight legs, plus the four legs for the hare.'

'I get you. I could have used that game when Charles was younger ... he was fractious ... intelligent, you see, got easily bored.'

'Yes ... well, me and Sara, we don't have that problem.'

'I'm sorry ... I didn't mean...'

'No matter, boss. So you keep adding up the legs. Saw a pub once called the Cricketers.'

'Apt.'

'Indeed ... so, eleven men in a cricket team, Jeremy had to multiply eleven by two to get the number of legs ... and that's the greatest ever number of runs scored by one pub sign, twenty-two.'

'Ah ... so the George and Dragon would be ... how many? Would you count the horse?'

'Probably, sir, he's often depicted as being on horseback ... so that would be ten legs; four for the horse, four for the dragon and two for George. Then eventually you'd see a pub called something like, The Three Horse

Shoes or the Cross Keys, no legs, so that's a wicket lost. Kept Jeremy amused on the way back from the coast last Saturday. Teaches him to observe the world around him and he has to do some mental arithmetic too. It's an excellent game for a long car journey with children.'

The remainder of the journey to Stamford Bridge was passed in relaxed and comfortable silence with Hennessey passing the time by indulging in a private game of car cricket and amassed eighteen runs from a Spotted Cow, a Fox and Grapes, a Grey Horse, a Mason's Arms, a Merry Monk and a Silent Woman, the sign of which pub showed a woman in medieval dress who, having been beheaded, was carrying her head under one arm. Eventually he was dismissed by a Royal Oak.

Approaching Stamford Bridge, Yellich slowed so that Hennessey could lean out of the window to enquire of a postman in a neatly pressed blue shirt and peaked cap the way to the Three Cranes. The only Three Cranes known to the postman was some three miles away in the next village and he proceeded to give clear and, as it transpired, perfect directions.

Yellich pulled into the car park of the Three Cranes, the sign of which showed three birds with elongated necks in graceful flight. The pub itself seemed a strange mixture of new and old. The building was old, half-timbered, red tiled roof, yet an extension had been added in grey brick and the car park was of the vast proportions associated with pubs built from the 1930s onwards. Hennessey, who had, over the years, developed a keen eye for reading the history of a landscape, felt that other buildings had been cleared from around the original pub to allow room for the extension and the generous car park. The pub stood at the edge of the village of Laytham Green, which appeared to be a quiet, linear settlement extending along either side of the main road but not greatly penetrating the hinterland. Once again, leaving the car windows open by a modest gap, the two officers walked across the car park to the pub and knocked on the door.

'They caught two German spies like this in the Second World War.' Hennessey turned and looked about him; fields of bronzed wheat stretched away to the skyline about a mile distant and were latticed with solid-looking hawthorn. Pleasingly traditional. He disliked landscapes where ancient hedge-rows had been ripped up to create American-style prairies and fields which were yellow with rape seed plants.

'Did they, skipper?' Yellich looked at him with interest.

'Apparently.' Hennessey turned back to face the door of the Three Cranes. 'Whatever else the Germans were good at in the war, it wasn't spying. They put two spies ashore at night from a motor launch, and these two guys paddled ashore in a small boat and then waded the last few feet and started walking ... this was in East Anglia.'

'Yes...?'

'Came to a village, saw a pub and knocked on the door ... this was about seven a.m. and the pubs didn't open until 11.00 a.m. at the earliest, like now, and anyway, the publican came downstairs in his nightshirt and these two Germans said, "You will sell to us some cider".'

'Oh no...'

'Oh yes ... hardly prepared. Anyway, the

publican gave them something to drink and then went to another room and phoned the police who arrived most promptly and whisked them away. Don't know what happened to them but I doubt that any more alcohol ever passed their lips.'

'Doubt it too, skipper. Ah...'

Hennessey heard it too, a footfall within the building, a turning of the key. He expected to be greeted with a 'Sorry we are not open yet', but instead a soberly dressed, short-haired woman, whose appearance and manner Hennessey thought could only best be described as bonny, smiled and asked, 'Can I help you, gentlemen?'

'Police.' Hennessey and Yellich showed their IDs.

'Yes? I hope there's no trouble.'

'So do we,' Hennessey replied with a smile. Yellich also smiled. 'We are really looking for information. Is the landlord available, please?'

'My husband? Yes...'

Hennessey glanced at the small licensee sign above the door. 'John Cochrane,' he read aloud. 'You'll be Mrs Cochrane?'

'Yes, I am.'

'You'll forgive me, but are you recent licensees?'

'Five years.'

'Ah ... well, probably no need to bother Mr Cochrane. We seek information about events some twenty years ago.'

'Twenty years ... I was still at school.' She wore a white blouse and black slacks, flat soled shoes; dressed for cleaning and polishing before the doors opened for the day's trade. 'You'll really have to talk to Fred Anglis, he was the licensee twenty years ago. My husband and I came from Hull ... we came to Laytham Green when we took the pub.'

'Is Mr Anglis living locally?'

'Unfortunately, yes.' Mrs Cochrane rolled her eyes. 'He's the bane of our lives. Comes in each evening at about six and won't let anyone forget he was the man ... or the gaffer as he calls himself. You know, "I did things this way ... wouldn't have that there ... wouldn't do things like this ... wouldn't tolerate that and, wouldn't ever be seen in my pub". He's getting well under our skins. I would have scratched him years ago, but John's a patient man, probably too patient

65

for a publican. He's my husband but he couldn't handle an inner-city pub ... but even John's getting to the end of his tether. I suppose it was his life for thirty years and now he's got nothing, so he's clutching at straws ... but it's our pub now ... he should respect that.'

'Seems so. Where do we find Mr Anglis ... did you say his name was?'

'Yes, Anglis.' She spelled it for the officers. 'Frederick Anglis. He has a house at the other end of the village, and I mean the other end, half an hour's stroll.'

'Half an hour?'

'It's two miles away, the village is long and thin, two miles from end to end ... just a line of buildings on one side of the road and a line of buildings on the other side, and hardly anything behind them.'

'Yes.' Hennessey nodded. 'I had that impression on the way here.'

'I run the length of the village each morning, from this end to that end and back. I run at about three times the normal walking pace and it takes me between twenty and thirty minutes there and back. So a half-hour's walk ... it's a pleasant stroll just depends how valuable your time is, gentle-men.'

'It's valuable. We'll drive.' Hennessey smiled. It was still the forenoon but he was already beginning to feel uncomfortable in the heat.

'Well, into the village and out the other end, large white house in its own grounds standing back from the road, called Blak-eney.'

'Blakeney, in its own grounds, not just a garden?'

'Well, there's good money in the licensed retail trade,' Mrs Cochrane said as she smil-ed. 'The work is hard and the hours are long but it's the thought of a house like Blakeney at the end of it all that keeps John and me going.'

Hennessey and Yellich thanked Mrs Cochrane and took their leave. Yellich drove slowly through Laytham Green, which to Hennessey seemed to have been little changed by the march of time. The motor vehicles said twenty-first century, as did the clothing on the few folk that were about, but the buildings themselves seemed to be little changed. There was a small supermarket with a large glass pane fronting on to the road, but beyond that the buildings were uniform, small, linked together and belonged to an earlier era. The shops had sun awnings and displayed their goods on the pavement outside; the houses were best described as cottages, thought Hennessey. The church had a square tower upon which flew the flag of St George, though on that day it hung limp against the blue sky. The headstones in the churchyard tilted this way and that, like a group of drunken sailors, having been stood in soil which had become unconsolidated by the excavation of the void.

Blakeney was easily found by Hennessey and Yellich being, as Mrs Cochrane had described it, large, white-painted and confidently squatting on a parcel of landscaped area large enough to be called grounds. A man in plus fours and a handlebar moustache was polishing a red MG circa 1950, which stood on a gravel drive outside a double garage. Hennessey and Yellich parked the car at the kerb and walked to the five-barred gate at the entrance to Blakeney. The man wearing plus fours glanced at them as they opened the gate and then looked away again. He carried on polishing the sports car until Hennessey and Yellich stood by the front bumper of the machine, encroaching his personal space.

'Help you gents?' he asked without looking at them, moving his arm in a slow, circular, purposeful manner as he polished the bonnet of the car. The chrome was already gleaming in the sun.

'Police,' Hennessey said and reached for his ID. Yellich did the same. 'Are you Mr Frederick Anglis?'

'Yes, I am, and there is no need for your IDs, I can tell a police officer. I worked in the licence retail trade all my life ... you get to tell people. I knew you were police officers as soon as you parked your car. So, how can I help you?' He stopped polishing and turned to face the officers. He was broad-shouldered, handlebar moustache, ruddy cheeks, bald with a rim of silver hair, over his ears. Very bushy eyebrows.

'We'd like to ask you a few questions, please.'

'Assumed you would. I have information you want, otherwise you wouldn't be here.'

'You think?'

'Well, you're not here to arrest me ... if you are it will be a wrongful arrest. I have things I feel guilty about but nothing that would interest the police. So, how can I help you?'

'You used to be the licensee of the Three Cranes in the village?'

'Used to be, that was my pub for thirty years. I intended to retire to Spain but in the end the roots had gone so deep I couldn't pull 'em up and so I stayed, also thought I would help that young couple find their feet. Nice couple, the Cochranes, but they have no idea how to run a pub. I'm going to live to see that place go to ruin. It would be worth something if they listened. There's nothing, nothing anybody can tell me about the licensed retail trade, nothing ... but they don't want advice. Will they listen? They don't have the attitude to be publicans ... that horrible extension ... turning it into a restaurant. You can either have a pub or a restaurant, but not both ... you get a kind of hybrid with children running about, but that's the way things are going these days ... all day opening ... no smoking ... maybe I retired at the right time.'

'The Dungeon Kings mean anything to you?' Hennessey pulled the conversation back to the investigation as a heavy bead of sweat ran from his hairline over the back of his right ear and dropped on to his collar.

'Oh, yes ... you're going back twenty years now. Bikers ... they were regulars.'

'Forgive me, but you don't seem the kind of publican that would tolerate bikers and the pub didn't seem to be the sort of pub they would want to go to ... it's a bit out in the sticks for a York gang.'

'Aye.' Anglis turned and rested both hands on the bonnet of his car. 'Well, it was my son who brought them ... he was a King. He went through his biker stage ... so I tolerated them in the garden. You know where the extension is?'

'Yes.'

'Well, there used to be tables and benches there, I let them drink outside but not in the pub. They came because Andrew was there and then only in the summer.'

'Andrew?'

'My son.'

'Ah...'

'Yes, he had some sway ... myself and Mrs

71

Anglis didn't like the gang but they called on Andrew, had a pint or two then roared away in the general direction of York.'

'I see ... so it wasn't their pub then?'

'No ... you have been misinformed there. The Kings, as they were, had some connection with the Three Cranes but it was not *their* pub in that sense. Sorry if you thought that. If you were told that then you've had a wasted journey.'

'Not at all wasted ... we need to talk to somebody who was in the gang. You said your son was a gang member?'

'Yes, a popular member, hence the reason why the gang called on him – like a swarm of roaring beetles in their black leathers.'

'Where might we find him?'

'He's got a pub of his own now ... followed me into the trade'

'Good for him.'

'Yes, massive place ... about as far as you can get from being a biker's pub, but then, he's also as far as you can get from being a biker ... it was just a stage he went through and came out unscathed ... those bikes ... awful machines.'

Hennessey winced inwardly. 'Did you

72

know any of the bikers?'

'None ... I never wanted to – didn't want to encourage Andrew's interest in them ... them, their machines and their chicks. The men didn't have girlfriends, they had chicks and when they came to the beer garden all the men sat together, and the biker chicks sat together, and the bikers ruled, that was obvious. The biker chicks just sat patiently waiting until the boys decided it was time to leave. I told you, I've been people-watching all my life, it's something you develop in the licensed retail trade.'

'Where would we find your son?'

'He's not in any trouble?'

'We don't think so.'

'You don't think so!' Anglis became hostile in his defensiveness. The sudden turning of attitude was, Hennessey had found, not uncommon among publicans, 'Hail fellow, well met' one second, aggressive the next. 'What's that supposed to mean?' Anglis demanded.

'It's not supposed to mean anything. It means just what we said; we don't think he's in trouble. We do want to chat to him about the Dungeon Kings.'

'He's the proprietor of the University Arms.'

'Being a pub?'

'Yes. It's close to the university in York on Heslington Lane in Fulford. I'll tell him to expect you, him and his *chick*.'

'That could be useful.' Hennessey smiled. 'We'll be there in about thirty minutes.' He paused. 'His chick?'

'Yes ... he married his chick ... his biker chick. Mrs Anglis and myself were ... we were dismayed when he brought her here, all leather and spiky hairstyle and studs in her nose. We knew great sadness that evening, but they moved on and on their wedding day she was as graceful and as elegant as any bride could be with her bridesmaids holding her train. Her father is a politician and he was just as saddened by his daughter's foray into the biker gang as we were saddened by Andrew's entry into it, but they both came through ... and we were delighted with the match and I think Robert is happy with his son-in-law.'

'Robert?'

'Robert Prendergahst.'

'*The* Robert Prendergahst, Minister for...'

'Trade and Industry? Yes, *the* Robert Prendergahst. His daughter Angela is our daughter-in-law ... delightful girl and now mother to our grandchildren. It was just a stage they went through ... those motorbikers ... just a stage ... nothing more than that.'

It was Tuesday, the eighteenth of June, 11.32 hours.

Three

Tuesday, 18 June, 12.15 hours –
Wednesday, 19 June, 01.35 hours
*in which a bedroom yields dark secrets and
both Ventnor and Webster are at home to the
gentle reader.*

'So, we've made some progress,' Hennessey
said as he glanced around his office. 'We still
have to get a positive match on the DNA
before we issue a press release, but I have a
pleasing sense of momentum. Well done.'
Yellich, Ventnor and Webster smiled and
nodded. 'This afternoon, Yellich and I will
visit Andrew Anglis at his place of work ...
the ... the...'

'University Arms, sir,' Yellich reminded
him.

'Yes, the University Arms. He's a living
link with the gang who called themselves the

Dungeon Kings ... but we don't know which pub they used. We'll find that out this afternoon when we talk to Andrew Anglis.' Hennessey drummed his fingers on his desktop. 'I'm going to stick my neck out ... the DNA will come back positive, it's going to be the body of Terence North. So ... Ventnor...'

'Yes, sir?'

'I want you to return to the Norths with this.' He opened his desk drawer and took out the sachet containing the gold hair clasp and laid it on his desk. 'Show this to the Norths ... see if they recognize it.'

'Yes, sir.'

'It is dulled, as you see, but it is gold ... not bronze ... the dullness comes with being in the ground for twenty years. They, or anyone else, might recall it as being shiny.'

'It wouldn't harm the investigation if it was polished up,' Ventnor suggested. 'I mean, if it was shining when it was buried with Terry North people would remember it that way. I would be happy to take it home and polish it up this evening. I have some polish.'

Hennessey paused. 'Yes ... you have a point, Ventnor ... so yes, do that ... but show the Norths as it is. It's a difficult day for them, two visits from us in one day, so I'll ask you to be as sensitive as possible.'

'Yes, sir, diplomacy is the word.'

'Good man. Now, Webster...'

'Sir?'

'I want you to hold the fort. The DNA results will come through by telephone in the first instance, followed by delivery of the document by courier.'

'Yes, sir.'

'When it comes ... as it will ... notify myself and Yellich. If we are still out of the building, you have our mobile numbers. Hate those brain fryers ... totally destroyed the romance of rail travel. I do resent having to listen to one half of a conversation.'

'It's fun when they're arguing, though,' Ventnor offered. 'Listening to one side of an argument can be fun.'

Hennessey scowled at him. He thought his flippancy inappropriate. 'But there is no disputing their usefulness at times. So, we all know what's happening?'

'Yes, sir.'

'Right ... well, an army marches on its stomach ... so does a police force. This is a good time to take luncheon. Yellich, you and I will rendezvous here in one hour's time.'

'Yes, sir.'

'Definite meeting tomorrow forenoon, here in my office, at 9.00 a.m. sharp, though we'll doubtless see each other before that.'

Hennessey signed out and, carrying his lightweight Italian-cut summer jacket over his arm with his wallet safely in his trouser hip pocket, and his Panama screwed on tightly against the overhead sun, he walked the walls from Micklegate Bar to Lendal Bridge, weaving in and out of foot passengers, all of whom, it seemed to him, to be walking in the opposite direction. Once again he was surprised that no one was bustled over the edge on the inner side of the wall, where the drop on to the grass bank was sufficient to cause fractures, especially in the frail elderly, and once again, he felt it high time for the city fathers to institute a one-way system on the walls, if only in high summer, when the tourists swell the population of York by many hundreds on any given day, and they all gravitate to the same places of interest. How strange, he thought, how these walls can be deserted and windswept and a few weeks later be obliged to carry an impressive volume of foot traffic.

He left the wall at Lendal, as indeed he was obliged to do because, unlike Chester where the medieval walls form a complete ring, Hennessey had found that York's walls were incomplete and comprise three separate sections. He crossed over Lendal Bridge, where the girls once used to solicit but had since moved indoors to the more comfortable, and safer, massage parlours. The pavement of the bridge was thronged with pedestrians, more so than the wall, and each mustered patience as their walk reduced to a shuffle as they stepped to one side and then the other, interweaving a path without cannoning another person into the roadway which itself was dense with traffic. He glanced at the Ouse, blue in the summer, invitingly cool-looking. A lemon-haired girl in a university T-shirt rowed a single scull with effortless grace and ease, keeping the oars perfectly in rhythm, the blades of the oars entering and leaving the water without, it seemed, the slightest disturbance. A red and white double-decker ferry, by brutal contrast, transported trippers for an excursion down the river, its diesel engine thumping out clouds of black smoke. Beyond was flat, green land and the skyline of distant houses, and a shrill whistle from the Railway Museum announced that a steamer had been fired and was taking passengers, mainly young families, in open wagons for a three-hundred-yard trip out of the museum on a track, parallel with the main line north to Newcastle and Edinburgh, and back.

Hennessey turned right into Lendal itself, passed the judges' residence, intending to dine at the fish restaurant, but at the last minute feeling fish and chips would be too hot and heavy on such a swelteringly hot day, drove deeper into the ancient city, down Davygate and Parliament Street. They were also crowded with tourists and buskers, who displayed varying talent, from the pale and sickly looking youth who managed to pick out 'Bobby Shafto' on a tin whistle, through to two young women with flowing hair and ankle length skirts who formed a violin duet and rendered perfect, so far as Hennessey's untrained ear could tell, executions of Mozart and Vivaldi. Jugglers and grease-painted human statues completed the scene. The recently introduced bye-law, that any person plying for money on the streets of York should be in possession of a street entertainer's licence, had enabled the police to rid the city of beggars, often young and with a puppy on the end of a length of string and who sat in front of a sign which said 'Hungry, homeless, please help'. They had not been missed nor fretted over, for, as Hennessey well knew, no one in the United Kingdom is homeless or hungry, save by their own choice. He turned left into Jubbergate and then right into the Shambles, where he found a quiet Italian restaurant and dined with great satisfaction on lasagne and salad. Ideal.

Hennessey returned via Micklegate, less thronged than the city centre, but he nevertheless still had to weave and wind his way through the pedestrian traffic. As he walked, he pondered the 'Micklegate Challenge' being to take a half pint of beer in every pub on the street; no one has been known to have managed it. He entered Micklegate Bar police station, signed in and opened the 'Staff Only' door and walked to the CID corridor. He found Yellich sitting at his desk reading the *Yorkshire Post*. 'Good lunch?'

'Good enough, skipper.' Yellich folded the newspaper. 'Police canteen stuff ... fills the gap.'

'Don't know how you can stand that muck.'

'It's cheap, sir ... that helps it go down more easily.'

'Well ... University Arms, it is, for we.'

'Yes, boss.' Yellich stood and reached for his jacket. 'Shall we walk?'

'No.' Hennessey shook his head. 'I know what you mean, hardly a car's journey, but it looks better if we arrive by car and we won't know what we're going to find ... we might need a vehicle.'

'Very good, boss.' Yellich grabbed his car keys.

The University Arms revealed itself to be a new-build red brick pub with the name in large gold lettering over the door. Half the car park was given over to tables and benches; probably, thought Hennessey, they would be taken in and placed in storage during the winter months, but in the summer they allowed customers to spill out and drink in the open air. Yellich halted the car by the front door of the pub, and he and Hennessey entered the building, which they found to be pleasantly cool and shady. It was nearly empty with just one or two, mainly elderly, people sitting in silent isolation. Hennessey and Yellich approached the bar and showed their ID to a young woman in a white blouse and black skirt.

'Mr Anglis, please.'

'He's upstairs ... I'll phone him.' She spoke in a southern accent and Hennessey assumed her to be a university student who was staying in York for the summer, like the single scull he had seen on the river before lunch. She turned and reached for a wall-mounted telephone that hung to one side of the spirit rack. She pressed a two-figure number and waited. 'He's not answering –' she half turned to the officers apologetically – 'but I know he's ... Ah ... Andrew ... Melanie here in the lounge. Two police officers to see you. No, they didn't say ... alright ... thanks.' She replaced the receiver and turned to the officers. 'He's on his way down.'

Hennessey smiled his thanks.

'My father said you'd be calling.' Andrew Anglis was tall, blond-haired, clean-shaven, sharply dressed in a suit and tie.

'Just information,' Hennessey explained. 'We're picking brains.'

'Ah ... well, anything I can do to help.'

'Is there somewhere we can go, away from the bar? There is a privacy issue.'

'Oh ... well, over here.' He indicated a darker corner of the lounge where chairs stood round tables. 'No one ever sits there unless they have to ... those seats only seem to get occupied if there's nowhere else to sit, which will be about eight hours from now ... dare say that ought to be enough time for you.'

'Dare say it will.' Hennessey inclined his head. 'After you, sir.'

Seated round the table, Hennessey believed he noticed a look of shock and perhaps worry cross the eyes of Andrew Anglis, as he explained the reason for his and DS Yellich's visit.

'Names from the past...' Anglis sat back in his chair. 'I never thought I'd hear those names again. Tony Wells ... and Terry North ... both no longer with us.'

'Yes.'

'But Tony's the same age as me ... he died in the hospice, too young ... and I just read yesterday that cancer is on the verge of becoming a chronic illness, something you live with rather than die from ... too late for Tony...'

'Well, yes, mid-forties is on the young side for cancer, but not unknown, sadly ... but it's really Terry North that we are interested in.'

'Yes ... Terry ... he disappeared. We never knew what happened to him ... until now.'

'And we still don't,' Hennessey said. 'We know that he died a suspicious death ... and was buried.'

'Yes...'

'So tell us about him. What manner of man was he?'

'Terry? A bit of an outsider ... in the gang ... not one of the leaders.'

'I gather you were?'

'A leader? No ... I, well both myself and Angela enjoyed popularity but I was not a leader.'

'Alright ... tell us first about Terry North ... then about the Dungeon Kings.'

'Terry ... not very popular on the outside...'

'Did he have a girlfriend?'

'Er ... yes ... yes, he did for a brief period, I seem to remember. Angela and I were not in the gang for a long time ... we were rebelling against very proper backgrounds. You've seen my father ... Angela's father is a politician ... a very senior politician now. In those days he was a middle bencher.'

'The Minster for Trade and Industry ... very impressive.'

'Not for long, according to the polls, the PM has to call an election in the next few months ... he could ask the Queen to dissolve Parliament any day now and the other lot look likely to get in. If that happens he's not going to be the minister for anything by Christmas.'

'So, did Terry work?'

'No ... he was a thief, he made a living by stealing ... he was a good burglar, very good at it ... he was never caught, or captured as he would say. He would talk about going on missions and avoiding capture ... soldier speak you see, it gave what he did some glamour in his eyes, some ... some ... honour

... It elevated it above thieving and house-breaking, but that's what he did. I've been burgled a few times and I have always been astounded how much stuff I have lost in terms of value.'

'Yes, it can add up.'

'All for about half an hour's work ... high risk – high yield. If you can't get work I can see the attraction in turning windows ... it clearly appealed to Terry.'

'You didn't get your hands dirty when you were a Dungeon King?'

'Well, I wouldn't tell you if I did ... but no ... neither me nor Angie did. We rode with them ... broke the speed limit with them, with the King chicks holding hands as the Kings rode side by side at a hundred miles an hour ... We did that, but as for committing crime when we were not with the gang ... no, we didn't, we didn't need to. A lot of the crime committed by members of the Kings was caused by lack of money. You can't run a 750cc bike on the dole ... and buy the helmet and leathers ... they had to go crookin' to afford it. They did drugs, burglaries and car jackings.'

'You could be prosecuted for withholding

information like that, even twenty years on,' Hennessey warned.

Anglis shook his head. 'It's just hearsay that I can offer, I have no hard evidence for you, even twenty years on. Twenty years? It's like a different lifetime, yet it also seems like yesterday.'

'So what do you know about Terry North's disappearance? Did he have any enemies?'

Both officers thought Anglis looked upset by the question; a look of discomfort cross-ed his eyes. It was there for a second, then gone, but it was there, and Hennessey and Yellich saw it.

'No ... I wouldn't say so ... mind you, I didn't really know Terry North, he wouldn't confide in me about enemies, if he'd had any.'

'Alright, tell us about his girlfriend.'

'Lass called Mandy ... Mandy ... what was her name? Fryston ... that was it, Mandy Fryston. Not the brightest button in the box ... never really talked to her.'

'Did your wife?'

'Angie? Yes, she would sit and chat. We used the same pub each Friday evening, the Dexter out on the road to Shipton. When we went there the blokes used to sit together and the girls would sit together ... so the "chicks" as they were called, would be able to tell you about Mandy Fryston. Unfortunately Angela is out, she's taken the children to visit her father.'

The officers noticed a tone of relief in Anglis' voice that his wife was not present to be interviewed.

'So,' Hennessey asked, 'how many were in the gang?'

Anglis shrugged. 'It varied ... members came and went ... some didn't get in, they failed the initiation.'

'Which was?'

'Sometimes their bike was too small, nothing less than 500cc was allowed. Others failed to do the circuit.'

'The circuit?'

'York, Beverley, Driffield, York ... has to be done in less than forty-five minutes ... about seventy miles.'

'Seventy plus miles in forty-five minutes!'

'Yes.' Anglis smiled. 'You can't do it without massively exceeding the speed limit, and it's not motorway driving, it's narrow country roads, straight in many places but plenty of blind corners. You get three attempts ... if you don't make it in three attempts, you don't get in. They time you out and time you back. You can't cheat because they check the mileage reading on your machine ... seventy-four miles. If it's substantially less then they know you've cheated, or more ... has to be seventy-four miles exactly. I did it on the second attempt. I would have done it on the first attempt but got caught up in traffic on the Beverley to Driffield leg. But to answer your question ... about twenty, that would be an average attendance at the Dexter, with about fifteen chicks. Not every biker had a chick.'

'I see. So what were the names of the gang members and where are they now?'

'The names? I can remember only a few ... mostly it was nicknames.'

'Nicknames will do as well.' Yellich smiled as he poised his pen over his notepad.

'Well, the Dungeon Master was a bloke called Hawson, Dickie Hawson, so I assume his Christian name was Richard.'

'The Dungeon Master?'

'The leader of the gang. We were all Dungeon Kings but he was the master, the

Master of the Kings.'

'Alright.'

'Then I remember a guy called Causey Jones ... never knew his first name. After that it was just nicknames that I used ... a lot of people were "mad"...'

'Mad?'

'The Mad Builder ... guy called Nick, Nicholas I assume ... he was in the building trade, then there was the Mad Accountant, he was going through his rebellious phase like me and Angie. He'll be an established professional now.'

'So they weren't all criminals?'

'No. I just remembered the Mad Accountant. What was his name? John ... John ... household item...'

'Household item?'

'Just the way my mind works, his surname reminded me of the inside of a house ... Bannister, John Bannister. He was the only other one in the gang that didn't have dirty fingers. Even though he was a biker, he had both eyes firmly on a career and he knew that any brush with the law would have finished him. Then I remember nicknames, Soldier and Ranker both military sounding

... then Animal. Then I remember the ones that gave motorbikers a bad name, The Streak ... he came off his machine at ninety miles an hour and made a hole in the side of a house. He didn't go all the way through but his body left a crater in the wall ... not much left of him. Ringer went the same way ... high speed blow out ... a farmer found his bike and his body probably a few days after the accident. Last seen on a Saturday, body found on Wednesday.'

'Well, we can let them rest in peace. What other names of the still living to recall...'

'Living at the time, you mean, Chief Inspector? No guarantee that they are alive now.'

'Point to you.'

'Spud Tate ... it's all coming back. Tate is short for potato from which you derive "spud". He was a very tall bloke, Spud ... bit too big for a bike. I really don't remember any other names. If I do I can call you.'

'Yes, please do.' He handed Anglis a card.

'Micklegate Bar? Oh yes, I know where that is ... red-brick building opposite the gate itself ... corner site.'

'Yes, that's it.'

'What about the girls, do you remember any of their names?' Hennessey persisted.

'No ... they were always known by their boyfriend's name, Soldier's chick, the Master's chick, the Mad Builder's chick...'

'I see. So we really will have to see your lady wife, Mr Anglis. I think we want to know about Mandy Fryston.'

'She'll be back tomorrow, if it can wait until then?'

'It can wait.' Hennessey stood. Yellich did likewise. 'It's a twenty-year-old murder, one day won't make a deal of difference.'

As they walked out of the University Arms and were hit by the weight of the heat of the sun, Hennessey's mobile vibrated in his pocket. He opened it and answered, listened, said, 'Thank you, you know what to do,' and replaced it in his pocket. 'That was Webster,' he said. 'Wetherby have come back with a positive match. The body is that of Terry North.'

'The press release will rattle a few cages.' Yellich unlocked the car.

'Which is what we hope. What did you think about him?' Hennessey nodded to the pub.

'Cagey,' Yellich said. 'I think he knows more than he's telling us.'

'I thought so too. You know we are going to come up against a wall of silence.'

'You think so, sir?'

'Yes ... the biker's code, "Don't grass on your mates". They are all still bikers in their hearts, early middle-aged as they may be. Once a biker, always a biker.'

Thompson Ventnor sighed and replaced his mobile phone in his pocket. He looked at Claude North and then at Edith and said, 'I'm sorry...'

'It's our Terry.' Claude North rested his hand on the table.

'Yes ... I am afraid so ... that was the police station, the results of the DNA test have just come back from Wetherby ... and yes ... I'm sorry.'

'When can we have the body? Find him somewhere proper to rest ... all those years in a clearing in a wood.'

'I'll let you know but I can't see why his body could not be released very quickly, the post-mortem has been completed.'

'You'll want to have a look at his room

now?'

'If you don't mind ... but first, can I show you this hair clasp?' He took it out from his pocket in its cellophane sachet and handed it to Mr North. 'Does that mean anything to you? Do you recognize it?'

'I don't ... do you, pet?' He handed it to his wife. Edith North took the sachet and examined the gold clasp. 'It's not a hair clasp ... only a man would think it's a hair clasp. It's a brooch ... worn on a coat lapel. Men! Yes, I do recognize it ... it belonged to that girl ... what was her name? He brought her home once or twice. A bit dull I thought ... hoped their relationship wouldn't last and it didn't. What was her name?'

'Mandy.' Claude North spoke with a certain finality. 'I remember because I've got a sister in New Zealand called Amanda ... she got called Mandy all her life.'

'Mandy ... aye ... this was her brooch ... solid gold, don't know where she got it ... must have cost a packet. Never knew what happened to her, last time we saw her was a few weeks before Terry went missing. He mentioned that he hadn't seen her for a while and she'd done a bit of a disappearing act, but we just assumed maybe they'd had a falling out. When Terry didn't come home, we didn't think about her at all.'

'You wouldn't,' Thompson Ventnor spoke consolingly. 'You wouldn't be expected to.'

'But ... it seems that the last we saw of her was about the time Terry disappeared.'

'That's true ... it was, wasn't it? It never occurred to me before but yes, there wasn't a long gap between the last time we saw Mandy and Terry disappearing,' Claude North added.

'You said he drove away on his bike?'

'Yes ... just like he did every Friday, meeting his mates in the motorcycle gang ... they met at a pub just outside York. Don't know which one it was, he never said.'

'Never said,' Mrs North echoed. 'We'll have to start phoning round ... folk will want to know ... funeral to plan.'

'Later, pet.'

'Aye, later.'

'Yes, he and his bike ... drove off ... never saw either again. The bike will be at the bottom of a river or will have been broken up for spares ... but that is of no interest. At least we know what happened to Terry. So you'll want to see his room, sir?'

'Yes, please'

Claude North led Thompson Ventnor to his late son's bedroom and halted at the door. He opened it and then stepped back. 'I'll leave you to it, sir. I'll go and be with my wife.'

Thompson Ventnor stepped into the room and stood just inside the doorway. The room was neatly kept, he thought, neater than his own house, and the open window gave it a quality of freshness, as though Terence had been allowed to live in the house, despite his long, long absence. Ventnor ventured further into the room and approached a chest of drawers. Starting at the bottom drawer he opened each drawer and probed among a young man's clothing and, finding nothing of interest, closed the drawers again. He opened the wardrobe and again found young man's clothing neatly hanging. The wardrobe had small pockets at one side, which contained a number of items, one of which was a small photograph album. Ventnor took it from the pocket and glanced through it. All the photographs seemed to be of a young man, his bike and his biker friends.

He placed the album on the bed and continued to search the shelves of the wardrobe. He found items that he expected to find, but not in the numbers he found them in: men's watches, for example, one, perhaps two but not the twenty-five he did find; and money, a few pounds, but not the many thousands of pounds, by then valueless, the type of note he found having long been withdrawn from circulation; and a tobacco tin contained degraded cannabis. He placed the watches, cash and cannabis on the bed beside the photograph album. Underneath the bed he found the pairs of shoes he expected to find. By then he was quite prepared to find anything at all, and was not surprised to find a parcel, the size of a house brick, tightly wrapped and sealed with masking tape. By its weight he thought it to be cocaine, possibly heroin. Whatever it was, it would have a substantial street value if it was uncut. In his experience, only uncut contraband is ever kept as tightly sealed as that package was. It had remained as it had been left because Mr and Mrs North wanted to keep their son's bedroom just so … in case he returned ... just in case one day a key was heard turning in the front door. Ventnor placed the items he believed germane into self-sealing cellophane sachets and left them on the bed. The photograph album he took to the living room and showed it to the Norths.

'Our Terry's book,' Mrs North explained.

'Do you recognize the people in the photographs?'

'Only the girl...' Mrs North turned the page. 'Here ... see, that's Mandy leaning on Terry's bike.' She handed the album back to Ventnor open at the page showing Mandy Fryston. She appeared small and round, Ventnor thought she had a vacant expression.

'I'd like to take this back to the station.'

'Of course. You'll let us have it back though?'

'Yes ... I'll give you a receipt for it.'

'Thank you.'

'I found one or two other items in his room ... I'd like to take them as well.'

'Yes ... anything.'

'Do you know what Terry kept in his room?'

'No.' Claude North walked over to the window and glanced out at Tang Hall. 'No, we had this rule ... we didn't go into each other's rooms. Edith might go in to clean and dust but she wouldn't open drawers or anything, so long as the boys, Terry and Roger, didn't bring anything home they shouldn't. If they didn't bring trouble to the door, we would respect their privacy.'

'I see ... and Roger ... he's not at home?'

'No, married with children ... his room has been cleared, you can go in if you like but there's nothing there.'

'No ... no ... that won't be necessary.' Ventnor smiled. 'I have found everything I am going to find ... I'm sure of that.'

'I'll get the package off to Wetherby,' Ventnor said, showing it to Hennessey back at the station, 'they can open it.'

'Yes,' Hennessey growled. 'So you had the same impression that Yellich and I gained?'

'The gang members have answers to many questions? Yes, sir, I did have that impression.'

Hennessey, Yellich, Ventnor and Webster stood in Hennessey's office in shirtsleeves drinking tea.

'The brooch was identified as belonging to Mandy Fryston.'

'Let's speak to her, she's probably Mandy something else now, but let's try and trace her. We really need to trace all the gang members, but Mandy would be a good place to start ... a good person to start with. She'll tell us things about Terry North that his parents wouldn't be able to tell us.' He leaned forward and tapped the keyboard of the computer on his desk and entered Mandy Fryston in the Criminal Records search engine. 'Oh, that is interesting.'

'What is, skipper?' Yellich drained his mug of tea.

'She, like her boyfriend, is no longer with us.'

'Oh?'

'Oh ... indeed. She was murdered about the time that Terry North was reported missing.' Hennessey reached for the file on Terry North. 'She was murdered just three weeks before Terry North was reported missing.'

'Was there a conviction, sir?' Webster asked.

'There was indeed ... one Harry ... blimey, where do they get these nicknames? Harry "the Horse" Turner ... sentenced to life, paroled after eight years ... last known address 24 Alwyne Place, Rawcliffe. He is to be visited, one very definite visit, Yellich and I will do that.' Hennessey glanced at his watch. 'We'll do that tomorrow. This has been a very productive day and the murder, as we have said, is a cold case. The trail has got as cold as it's going to get, no need to push the overtime limit on this one. So, what's for action?'

'Trace all known and surviving gang members, sir.' Webster once again sounded enthusiastic.

'Yes ... that's a job for you.'

'I'll get the package off to Wetherby, sir,' Ventnor offered.

'Yes, that won't take long, then tee up with Webster on tracing the gang members ... Of the gang, I really think we need to find Hawson, the gang leader, the so-called Dungeon Master. He will still have an overview of the gang ... he'll be a useful person to chat to, if he'll co-operate.'

'If they have stayed in the crime pond,

they won't co-operate, boss,' Yellich offered. 'The best way in is to approach those who were on the fringes and then left to pursue careers. Anglis, for example, we both feel he was hiding something. He would be more likely to fall over if leaned on, and didn't he mention a Mad Accountant ... fella called Bannister?'

'Yes ... yes, he did.'

'If he has become an accountant, he too wouldn't relish a visit from ourselves.'

'Well, we'll see what we see, but I think you're right ... the soft underbelly of the gang will be those few who went on to become professional people.' He turned to Webster. 'See who is known before you leave for the day ... have a list for you and Ventnor to work through tomorrow. And you, Ventnor, you get that package off to Wetherby right away.'

'Yes, sir.'

'So we all know what we are doing? Here, my office, at 9.00 a.m. tomorrow.'

Reginald Webster drove home to Selby. He enjoyed the drive; he found the pleasant rural landscape very soothing with its flat green fields and the occasional stand of trees. He liked the small villages like Crockey Hill and Reighton on the more direct and speedier A19, but on that day, feeling relaxed, he opted for the slower route home along the B122 and approached Selby via Cawood and Wistow. He turned into his driveway and sounded the car horn twice then twice again, in the knowledge that he was committing a road traffic offence, but his wife had higher needs, higher priorities than the nuisance caused by sounding the horn of a stationary vehicle. He left his car and approached the house and as he did so the side door opened and a tall, fair-haired woman stood on the threshold, holding out her arms and smiling. He took hold of one of her arms and she, finding his body by touch, allowed herself to be drawn into his embrace.

He did not allow her to prepare hot food but she had managed to prepare a hearty and filling cold supper which they ate together in fond silence, with her having put effort into her appearance to please her husband, and he, once again, finding himself deeply moved, humbled by the courage she displayed.

He was very, very proud of her.

Gillian Stoneman looked at the ring, a huge, she thought, huge diamond encrusted with emeralds. She moved her finger to make it glint in the candlelight. She slid her hand across the table and met it with his.

'Happy?' he asked.

'Close to tears happy.' She held eye contact with him. 'Spoke to a patient yesterday ... he told me not to wait too long ... he said that that was the mistake he had made in his life.'

'What did you say?'

'Nothing really. I just thought of you and said, "Time yet". It was his space anyway, he had things to talk about, he had issues to resolve ... it wasn't for me to talk about myself.'

'Divorced,' Ventnor explained. 'Not fully finalized yet, but as good as. Have to sell the house still.'

'Oh.' The woman in the tightly clinging scarlet dress smiled but the smile had a certain insouciance.

He had driven the short distance home to his house in Bishopthorpe and glanced once at the untidy garden and had convinced himself that it didn't need attention yet. He let himself into his house, which was similarly grimy and had developed a musty smell as the summer had become established. He vacuumed occasionally and dusted, also occasionally, but could never seem to get on top of the housework in the same efficient manner his wife had been able to do. He bathed, changed into clothing and went into York and walked from pub to pub having a beer in each until he finally fetched up at the Augustus Nightclub for their 'over twenty-fives' night and sat at the bar next to the woman in a clinging scarlet dress.

'Me too,' she said, 'messy business, but second best I say ... though in my case it will be third best.' She allowed him to buy her a glass or two of expensive wine, but as usual he found he went home alone.

He thought about what Yellich had told him, seventy-four miles in forty-five minutes on country roads – that was some ride.

It was Wednesday, the nineteenth of June, 01.35 hours.

Four

The man glanced once at Hennessey and Yellich as their car drew up outside his house and then recommenced digging with a garden fork, bayoneting the soil and then twisting with what seemed to Hennessey to be both an angry and a practised hand. He glanced beyond the man to the house, a low whitewashed bungalow, tiled roof. The next nearest house was a similar bungalow a hundred and fifty yards away; the next nearest house to that was in the village. Beyond the bungalow Hennessey noticed wide lush green pasture where a herd of Herefords were contentedly grazing; a heron glided across the blue and near cloudless sky. Hennessey and Yellich got out of the car

108

and walked up to the wooden gate of the bungalow and pushed it open. 'Harold Turner?' Hennessey asked.

'Yes. What is it now? Whatever it is, I don't do it.' He carried on digging, turning the sods with mechanical thoroughness. He wore boots, shorts and a T-shirt; a hat protected him from the sun. He was tall and sinewy, little spare flesh. Prison life does that to a man, Hennessey observed.

'Just information. We were told you'd be here.'

'Yes ... my old man phoned to warn me to expect you. I don't live in Rawcliffe any more. You can put this down as my address so you don't have to bother my old man again ... he's getting on. I'm 46 now and I was a late baby. He's in his eighties now; he doesn't need bother from you. He's earned a quiet life ... leave him alone.'

'We will. Are you happy to talk here or shall we go inside?'

'Who said we're talking? Who said we are going to talk? Who said I was happy talking to the law?' He continued to dig.

'We're here in connection with the murder of Terry North.'

'Thought you would be.'

'What do you know about it?'

'Nothing.'

'You expected us, though?'

'Saw the report on the news. Then my old man phoned and said you were looking for me. Always did wonder what happened to North ... now I know ... but that's one murder you can't pin on me. I was inside when he disappeared ... on remand.'

'For the murder of Mandy Fryston.'

Harold Turner said nothing.

'We are looking for the gang members of the biker gang ... the Dungeon Kings.' Yellich attempted to prompt a response.

'Look around you.' Turner waved his hand as if indicating the expanse of the area round his bungalow. 'That's where you'll find them ... scattered to the four winds.'

'Mandy Fryston was Terry North's girlfriend ... so why did you kill her? Was there a quarrel?'

Harold Turner continued to turn the sods as if savouring his reply. 'I didn't kill her.'

'You changed your stance when you were convicted...'

'Aye ... started to work for an early parole

... some wrongful convicts have another attitude, just won't admit to something they haven't done ... but that's their right and sometimes they get a judicial review but by then the damage is done, by then they've been in category A or B prisons for twenty years. No one can survive more than ten years in high security ... it breaks you –' he tapped the side of his head – 'breaks you in here. So I started to work for a parole ... admitted guilt ... and was a model prisoner, got re-assessed from Cat A to Cat B and then to Cat C within five years, then the last three years were in Catterall.'

'Open prison.'

'Yes, a holiday camp ... pre-release programmes ... kept my mind thinking independently ... that's why I'm not under the Ouse Bridge with a bottle for company or a permanent resident with the Salvation Army. I can manage money and shop ... and here ... look, I'm planting potatoes ... "digging for victory", like in the war. What use is a front lawn when you can grow food? Did you know the English invented the lawn?'

'Confess I didn't.'

'The knack the English have of turning a

disadvantage to an advantage ... they took a weed, that is grass, and used it to create a lawn ... pretty soon everybody in Europe wanted lawns and there were spin-offs ... croquet was invented, as was bowls, as was tennis. Didn't waste my time inside ... did an Open University degree ... a few foundation courses and then focused on history ... loved it ... that really did keep me sane but I can't get work, no one will employ a man with a murder conviction. But I survived the pokey ... kept my head together.'

'It read like a safe conviction.' Hennessey brushed a fly from his face.

'You think so?' Harry Turner glanced at Hennessey. 'No witnesses ... no motive.'

'She was stabbed to death, the murder weapon with your fingerprints on it was found near the murder scene ... her blood was found on the handgrips of the handlebars of your bike. Sounds safe to me.'

Harry Turner shrugged. 'I didn't recognise the knife, but anyone could have planted it outside the house. Then I lived in a drum in Holgate, kept my bike outside, anyone could have dipped the knife in her wounds, get it covered in blood holding it so as not to smudge the prints ... then dropped it near the body. Anyone could have smeared a bit of her blood on my bike as though it had come from my hands. She bled a lot, the murderer would have been covered in her blood, but there was no blood on my clothes.'

'It was a week or two before you were arrested ... time to destroy all the clothes you were wearing that night.'

'Yeah ... that's another thing ... how come they arrested me? I must have been the only one in the Dungeon Kings not to have a record. My prints were not on file, yet the cops came to my door ... they took my bike away, found traces of her blood on the hand grips ... arrested me, charged me ... took my prints. I had no alibi so I was done for it. Somebody fingered me for that. I was set up and then fingered. I got my name because I had a laugh like a whinnying horse. I haven't laughed in a long time. I still think I was right to admit to the murder ... doing so enabled me to survive and I got a good degree which didn't cost me anything ... the Home Office picks up the fees ... but I still lost eight good years, lost half of my twenties, first few years of my thirties, years when I really should have been enjoying life before settling down. Those days won't come again ... and I can't use my degree for anything. So I took the rental on this bungalow and dig the garden. I'm turning the garden into a large vegetable patch, that way I can afford a bit of meat now and again.'

'So, why don't we start working towards the same end?'

Turner looked at him curiously. 'Meaning?'

'Well ... suppose we agree to keep an open mind about the validity of your conviction. I mean, no promises, but you can only help yourself. The murder of Terry North and Mandy Fryston must be linked ... they were an item ... you're in the clear for one of them.'

'If you were to get your conviction overturned,' Yellich explained, 'not only would you be in line for a large sum of money as compensation for wrongful imprisonment, but your name would be removed from the criminal register and you could use your degree ... make a career for yourself.'

'Would that be possible?'

'Yes.' Hennessey smiled. 'It would be possible … but no promises.'

'Well, it's hot out here.' Turner drove the fork into the soil and let it remain upright. 'The sun's fierce. Why don't we go inside?'

'Some view.' The man followed Webster's gaze out of his living room window.

Webster turned away and smiled. 'Yes.'

'Daily reminder of where we are all going.' Nicholas Sitwell glanced at Fulford Cemetery that stood on the opposite side of the road to his modest council-owned home. 'But it's quiet in the evenings and I think I'd rather look at the gravestones than another house. These houses opposite the bone yard are not popular because of the view, but we like it. Anyway, take a seat.' He sat in an armchair.

'It's about Terry North.' Webster sat opposite in a second armchair, Ventnor sat on the settee.

'Assumed it would be, saw the news … did wonder what happened to him … knew it couldn't be good.'

'Oh?'

'Well, young man disappears in a city like

York. I mean, a civilised place, and I remember Terry was a bit dim ... not a clever lad ... a follower ... I didn't really know him.'

'Other people have said that.'

'Well, that's Terry, put up with ... what's the word? Tolerated ... tolerated rather than belonging. But from what I did know of him, I didn't think he would have the nous to disappear to start a new life, so I knew it was a bit iffy when he vanished. He stopped turning up for meets ... you couldn't do that.'

'Do what?'

'Leave ... there's an initiation, a test of bike driving skill.'

'So we heard.'

'Well, you couldn't join easily and you couldn't leave easily. Not without a good reason. We kept it tight, even for the hangers-on like Terry North. We went round to his house ... he hadn't shown for two weeks, so we went round and his old mum was wringing her hands with worry. She was pleased to see us in case we knew where he was but we didn't. So he was in a shallow grave all along ... knew it was bad.' Sitwell was neatly dressed in casual summer clothing, white slacks, bright coloured short-sleeved shirt. His home was inexpensively but neatly furnished, with souvenirs from Spanish holiday resorts in full view. 'So, how did you find me?'

'Well, your name was mentioned as being part of the same motorcycle gang that Terry North belonged to.'

'Yeah.' Sitwell's eyes gleamed and he made the motion of riding a motorbike. 'Those days ... I grew out of them. I started to slow down going round corners and lost my appetite for fights ... so I bought myself out, told the Dungeon Master I just wasn't up to it, I wasn't keeping up with the pack. I was getting to feel I'd be a liability in a scrap with another gang. He was OK about it ... so we left the bikes at home and met at a pub and got drunk and I paid for it all. That was an expensive night for an electrician but they'd speak to me when we saw each other ... wave when we passed each other on the street and that's what Terry should have done, which is why we knew that it was iffy, that he didn't show for two weeks.'

'I see.'

'Well, you're in our records. Nicholas

Sitwell a.k.a. the Mad Builder.'

'Yeah ... I was actually a sparky not a brickie but the name stuck. I should have been the Mad Sparky.' He paused. 'So I'm still on file? I thought convictions were spent after seven years?'

'It depends on the conviction, yours are spent ... won't be taken into account if you re-offend, but we keep records.'

Nicholas Sitwell shook his head. 'Tried to save a bit of money by buying shoplifted items. I was done for receiving stolen goods ... the fine was ten times more than I saved. Then a few convictions for speeding and causing an affray, but I can live with them ... they're proper bikers' crimes ... manly ... but I don't want my lads to go down that road. One of them got brought home by the police and was let off with a warning. He was loitering with intent ... probably acting as a lookout for a gang that was turning windows. Anyway, I gave him such a hiding that I thought I'd have those child welfare busies at my door. I want him to do well in life, and you don't do well by getting known to the police.'

'So, Terry North?'

'Terry ... aye ... not much I can tell really, just stopped coming.' The man avoided eye contact with Webster. 'Always wondered what happened to him, now I know ... shallow grave ... aye.'

Webster paused. 'You've got a nice home here, Mr Sitwell.'

'Yes.'

'And a family?'

'Wife and two sons, both good boys.'

'Self-employed?'

'Bus driver ... that is long distance motor coach. Got a P.S.V. licence and gave up the sparks ... still got me tools ... I could go back to it but I like driving ... I see Britain. Up to Scotland tomorrow, then across to Blackpool on Friday ... a pensioners' day out, poor tippers but at least they won't be sick on the way home. Next week I'm running holidaymakers down to Torquay ... Devon. One day down there, night in a cheap hotel ... back up the next day with an empty bus. Love those long journeys when the bus is empty, listening to what I want to listen to on the radio, coming home clean, not covered in muck.'

'Yes, I see your point, but will you see

mine?'

'Which is?'

'That you've got a lot to lose.'

'How will I lose anything? I've turned the corner, got responsibilities...'

'By withholding information.' Ventnor leaned back in his seat on the settee. 'Terry North might have been murdered twenty years ago but the person or persons that did this will still go down for life.'

'As will any accomplice,' added Webster.

'You see, it doesn't ring true, Mr Sitwell.'

'What doesn't?'

'Your story ... you used the word manly to describe your crimes ... Terry North's death was manly ... his cause of death was very manly, he was beaten to death. The post-mortem results were very clear ... bones broken everywhere ... then buried in his biking leathers...'

'That's biker sort of manly.' Webster leaned forward. 'We'll find out who did what ... we'll find out who is not telling what...'

Sitwell paled.

'So it's in your interest to co-operate, Mr Sitwell.'

Sitwell remained silent. 'I've told you all I

know,' he said at length. 'All I know. He just didn't turn up for a meet. Disappeared.'

'Well, just think about it.' Webster stood. 'There is one member of the gang we would like to trace, the man who was known as the Mad Accountant. What do you know about him?'

'Nothing.' There was a trace of fear in Sitwell's voice.

'Sure?' Webster raised his eyebrows. 'You see we have a list here...' He took his notepad from his pocket. 'Names you may remember: Causey, Soldier, Ranker, Animal, Spud, Harry the Horse, The Beast, the Dungeon Master, and Coffin Dodger.'

'They're all known to us except Andrew Anglis whom we have visited, and except the member of the Dungeon Kings who was known as the Mad Accountant. We're visiting all the names. One or two didn't turn the corner like you and are in the slammer. Soldier has collected twenty years for armed robbery.' Webster raised his eyebrows. 'He'll want to chat.'

'I know ... I heard.' Sitwell still looked pale.

'So, we'll find the Mad Accountant and

when we do, if we find out you knew where he is, we'll be back and you'll be coming with us ... charged with obstruction.'

'That's the least you can expect.' Ventnor also stood. 'Anything you want to tell us about him?'

'I don't know where he lives. He was a bit posh, he left after a couple of years.'

'He was a member when Terry North was murdered?'

'Yes. All I know is his name ... Bannister.'

'Bannister.' Ventnor smiled. 'Good.' He took a card from his pocket, which he handed to Sitwell. 'My name and phone number are on there. You can work against yourself or you can work for yourself. Anytime you want to start working for yourself ... just pick up the phone.'

Driving away from Sitwell's house, Webster said, 'Well, that confirms what Anglis said, Bannister is the name of the Mad Accountant. He won't be difficult to find if he's practising in York. The boss is right, he and Anglis are the ones to lean on. The others will be like Sitwell ... he was holding something back.'

'Wasn't he just? Might be interesting to

meet the Dungeon Master, see what he has to say. Where is he?' Ventnor slowed in readiness to join the main road.

Webster consulted the list he and Ventnor had compiled that morning. 'Oh ... he's a guest of Her Majesty, he's in Full Sutton. Five years for wounding.'

'So how does this work? I help you, you help me?' Harry the Horse Turner sat opposite Hennessey and Yellich. The inside of his bungalow was cool, pleasantly so, though Hennessey felt it would be difficult to heat in the winter months. The bungalow was sparsely furnished and decorated. It seemed to both officers to be the home of a man who has money for rent, food and fuel, and for little else.

'Sort of.' Hennessey sat back in the chair that he found lumpy, uneven and uncomfortable. 'You could start by telling us who you think killed Mandy Fryston ... if it wasn't you.'

'This is going to be the difficulty; I am trapped by the bikers' code.'

'Which says?'

'That you don't rat out another biker ...

plain as that. Simple as that.'

'But you can't be bound by the bikers' code if you are no longer a biker ... if the biker gang no longer exists and if it could have saved you from a murder conviction.'

'Even so ... once a biker, always a biker. I'll be a marked man. The biker who grasses on his mates ... other biker gangs will target me. I won't be safe. I'll have to move to another area of the country ... but all I've ever known is Yorkshire ... and taking the rap for a crime I didn't commit, well, that's for the other guy to step forward to prevent that, not for me to grass him up ... and if he doesn't step forward, then down I go.'

'So, where do we go from here?' Hennessey appealed to Turner. 'I mean, if you won't talk to us, how can we help you?'

Turner smiled. 'I never said I wouldn't talk to you. If I give you information, it didn't come from me. If you're pointed in the right direction, I didn't do the pointing.'

'Understood.'

'And I won't give evidence.'

'I can't guarantee that ... we could enforce your testimony in court.'

'I'd just refuse ... even if I go down for

contempt.'

'Well, alright...' Hennessey began to become intrigued. 'We'll do what we can to avoid that.'

'Not good enough, we'll avoid it completely.'

'Let's just see where we get ... and it didn't come from you.'

'Well, you should look at the Dungeon Master.'

'The headman?'

'Yes ... Richard Hawson ... known as Dickie or Dick ... Dick usually. Dick Hawson.'

'Why?'

'Because he will know who murdered Mandy Fryston. I don't think he did it himself ... he was fly like that, clever. Very careful not to let himself get involved with anything illegal ... no ... I don't mean that.' Harry Turner sat back in his chair. 'How to put this? He was involved, up to his neck ... but the law wouldn't be able to prove anything.'

'We know the type.'

'Well, he's like that. If the guy who murdered Mandy ... or guys ... were in the

Dungeon Kings, then they were above me in the pecking order ... in the hierarchy ... and I was middle ranking. Anybody lower or the same level as me would be told to give themselves up to the law to stop me going down for the murder.'

'So who was above you?'

'The Dungeon Master himself ... Dick Hawson ... then there was Animal, Soldier, Ranker, and the Mad Accountant.'

'The Accountant?'

'Yes ... the Master took a liking to him, even though he wasn't a biker, not in his heart. He played at it for a year or two, but when Mandy Fryston and Terry North were topped, he was in the inner circle. He might have been middle class from a private school and university, but he did the seventy-four and he was handy to have around in a fight.'

'I see.'

'We'd go out for a burn-up into the Dales ... riding two-by-two ... like an army display team. Dangerous really, like a pack, the other bike just a foot away from you on one side ... less ... the bike in front just inches away from your tyre, the bike behind just inches from your rear wheel, travelling down country roads like that, sixty, seventy miles an hour ... but the trust that that involved ... If one rider messed up, especially at the front, the whole gang would crash ... the Kings bonded like that; all biker gangs do ... with the chicks on the pillion, holding hands with the chick on the next door bike. But when we rode like that there was a place for each biker. It wasn't random, the Master and Animal were usually the first two machines ... then Soldier and Ranker, then the Mad Accountant ... and he'd usually team up with Camel. Then after them the guys who were middle ranking would team up in two's, any two, it didn't matter, they made up the bulk of the gang, then the last four bikers were the poor guys at the bottom of the pecking order ... people like Terry North.'

'Interesting.'

'Oh, yes, there's more to a gang of bikers than meets the eye.'

'So...' Hennessey's voice faltered as a low rumble filled the room, growing so loud that speech was impossible.

'From the base,' Harry Turner said apologetically. 'The RAF base, it's about ten miles from here but you'd think it was in the next field, they come down so low when they are landing. Taking off, they climb steeply, that's not so bad but landing ... they make jugs in the kitchen rattle. He was landing ... or she ... they have females flying fast jets these days.'

Hennessey began to warm to Turner, just a little, but warm nonetheless. He'd been wrong about people before, but Turner did seem genuine. 'So, if you are being truthful, what you are saying is that one of the top five members of the Dungeon Kings could have murdered Mandy Fryston and left you to carry the can?'

'Yes ... one, or all five ... anyone who rode behind those six in the pack could be sacrificed to the law to enable the other six to escape. The King, he'd escape, and anyone who was valuable to him, he would also escape ... anyone else could be sacrificed. Easiest thing in the world to creep down our street one night and smear Mandy Fryston's blood on my handlebars ... get hold of a knife with my prints on it. We used to carry knives, show each other our blades ... I remember admiring a few blades like that. Anyone could have owned the blade used to murder Mandy. I was shown it in court and earlier at the police station. I didn't recognize it but since I was denying everything, well ... it didn't seem to count for much that I claimed not to have recognized the blade.'

'So, this man Hawson ... he'll have the overview?'

'I reckon.'

'Why would he want her murdered?'

Turner shrugged. 'Don't know how far it ever went. Just before I was banged up, the Master was getting into crime ... like organized crime ... using the gang members as couriers.'

'For controlled substances?'

'Yes. Hull docks to York on a 750cc is less than an hour ... much less ... thirty minutes. London to York on a 750cc is about an hour and a half ... a couple of pounds of pure, uncut heroin in the pannier ... worth a million or so on the street. Then it was heroin ... now it would be crack cocaine. Could even have been ordinary cannabis.'

'He was distributing the stuff?'

'No...' Turner shook his head. 'Like I said,

he was too fly ... but he would hire out the members as couriers. You know there are courier firms – cycle and motorcycle – carrying high value but very low bulk items at speed, if there was time pressure. You know ... film of a breaking news item that's got to get to the BBC before the 6.00 p.m. news?'

'Yes.' Hennessey nodded. 'I know those companies. They're very useful ... we use our own motorcycle couriers.'

'Well, I wasn't in the inner circle but the boys were talking about becoming couriers for the Dungeon Master, picking up a package someplace ... delivering it to an address someplace else ... get handed a sealed brown envelope in return that you hand unbroken to the Master. He gives you a cut and no one asks questions. He was contracting out the gang to the underworld, but using the serfs before he used his princes.'

Hennessey and Yellich glanced at each other but said nothing.

'You look like you know something,' Turner pressed.

'We might, but we ask the questions.'

'Alright.' Turner held up his hand. 'Sorry.'

'So, of these five –' Hennessey consulted the notes he had made – 'Animal, Soldier, Ranker, the Mad Accountant, and Camel ... which ... who do you suggest we approach, if the Master is too fly, as you say, too fly for us to get near him?'

'None of them.' Turner smiled.

'None?'

'No ... I'd look up a girl ... a woman now, called Janet ... Janet...' Turner drummed his fingers on the arm of the chair in which he sat. 'Janet Middleton ... that's it ... Janet Middleton ... slender ... good looking girl.'

'Janet Middleton.' Hennessey wrote the name in his notebook. 'Who is she?'

'She be the one time girlfriend of Animal. He got tired of her so he sold her for ten nails.' Turner shrugged. 'Sorry, but that's the way it was ... in all biker gangs ... the chicks were low value. Find her ... she's got a record. Anyway, she wanted out after that.'

'I don't blame her.'

'But for a chick to leave the gang involves more than buying all the beer for an evening...'

'What happens?'

'I'd rather she tell you that.'

131

★ ★ ★

Richard Dickie Hawson, a.k.a. the Dungeon Master, revealed himself to be thin and muscular with piercing cold blue eyes and arms patterned with self-administered tattoos. 'So, what do you want?' He leaned back in his chair and eyed Webster and Ventnor with cold-eyed suspicion. 'The cops only ever visit a lag if they want something. So, tell me, what do you want?'

'Information.'

'What's in it for me?'

'Who knows? Help will be noted ... it would count towards an early parole.'

Hawson snarled. 'I'm three to five stretch ... I'm due for a parole hearing any day. I haven't been a bad lad ... no disciplinaries against me. I'll be walking in a few weeks. You need something more than that to make me want to help you.' He paused. 'Anyway, I'm clean.'

'You are?'

'Yes ... I have a few priors ... tame stuff ... but the judge thought the attack on the guy was serious enough to warrant five years ... so, here I am working towards a three ticket.'

'Serious? You nearly decapitated him. We read the file ... he is lucky to be alive. You nearly killed him ... he's traumatized for life. Some would say a five stretch is lenient.'

Hawson smiled as if complimented. 'He shouldn't have stared at me like that. The guy just didn't know how to go on in pubs ... reckon he does now.'

'Terry North.' Webster spoke suddenly.

'Mandy Fryston,' Ventnor added.

Hawson's eyes narrowed. The names meant something to him, more than simply people he had known twenty years ago.

'You're going back a long way.' A cautious tone entered his voice. He seemed to lean further back, further away from the officers. Both officers felt that the names held a chilling significance for him.

'You don't watch the news or read the papers?'

'Sometimes.'

'Recently?'

'No ... not recently.'

'So you don't know about Terry North?' Ventnor pressed.

'No ... what about him?'

'He's turned up ... at least his body has.'

'Terry's dead? Oh, I am sorry to hear that.'

'You don't sound sorry.' Ventnor eyed Hawson.

'Still less do you sound surprised,' Webster added.

'I remember Terry ... a good lad ... a bit short up here, you know –' he tapped the side of his head – 'but a nice enough lad. That was in the days of the Dungeon Kings ... good days.'

'So we understand. And you were the Dungeon Master?'

'Yep ... I was the man.'

'So, what happened to the gang?'

Hawson once again shrugged. 'Faded and scattered.'

'Didn't do so well for yourself, did you?'

Hawson's eyes narrowed. The comment had clearly stung him. 'What do you mean?'

'Well, each and every time you've been arrested you have described yourself as un-employed. Now you're in your forties and you are doing time ... Category B ... They're keeping their eyes on you.'

'I was Cat A ... I worked down to Cat B.'

'Interesting that you say down to Cat B. I would have said up to Cat B ... it's progress.'

'Up, down ... it's still progress ... the same ... all progress, all to impress the parole board with,' Hawson commented.

Webster took a packet of cigarettes from his jacket pocket and offered one to Hawson, who snatched it. He put it between his lips and leaned forward as Webster lit a disposable lighter and held it to the tip of the cigarette.

Hawson inhaled deeply. 'You don't know how much this is worth. We get rationed ... an ounce a week ... you get through that in a day. Rest of the time you're gasping and gagging ... unless you're a tobacco baron ... offering protection to other lags in return for their ration, but even the barons can't make it through the week ... not the full seven days.' He inhaled again. 'So, this is really ... really appreciated.' Again he inhaled. 'I didn't smoke until I got banged up ... then it replaces booze ... you kill time on the outside by going to the pub ... you kill time on the inside by smoking.'

'Well, I have a whole packet here.' Webster tapped the side of his jacket, over the pocket. 'If you have the inclination.'

'The inclination?' Hawson inclined his

head and blew smoke rings. Ventnor was impressed by the height they gained before dissipating.

'To co-operate.'

'Co-operate?'

'Yes, instead of steering the conversation into safe areas like tobacco barons and your smoking habit ... and back to the murder of Terry North.'

'He was murdered?' Hawson did attempt to hide his mock surprise.

'Yes, he was murdered.'

'Oh...' Hawson smiled. 'Who did it?'

'That's why we are visiting you, plying you with tobacco because we know that you know who killed him.'

'I do?' Hawson raised his eyebrows.

'Yes ... you were "the man", the leader, The Dungeon Master ... He was murdered wearing his biker gear.'

Hawson gave a single shrug. 'Means nothing.'

'It means biker.'

'The gang turned on him. If he had been attacked by a rival gang, his body wouldn't have been buried and there would have been retaliation. We would have had a biker gang feud on the streets of York.'

'But that didn't happen –' Ventnor leaned forward – 'so it was in-house ... the Dungeon Kings turned on him, battered him to death and buried the body.'

'You think?'

'No ... we know ... Tony Wells told us.'

'Tony ... Tony the Pig Wells ... that Tony Wells?'

'Yes.'

'The rat!' Hawson's face twisted with hatred, he clenched his fists until his knuckles whitened. 'The swine ... that's against the code ... ratting on his mates. What did he get in return? Reduced charges for something?'

'No ... he got it off his chest.'

'That's all he wanted to do ... just get it off his chest before he died,' Webster added.

'The Pig's away?' Hawson relaxed a little.

'Yeah.' Webster nodded. 'The Pig's away ... in a hospice ... the Big C. Last thing he did before he croaked was to tell a member of staff where we'd find a body and she told us.'

'And we are here,' Ventnor added. 'It seems that it was only hours before his own death that he realized the need for a grave ... not for the occupant ... but the surviving relatives.'

'Soft cretin.' Hawson drew on the cigarette. 'He wasn't the hard man he thought he was and this proves it. Just had to open his gob ... just couldn't take it to his grave ... and give us all peace ... soft as putty.'

'So we know it was the Dungeon Kings who were at the bottom of this, he was a King, so was Terry. The body was buried so it wasn't down to a rival gang. So, what do you know?'

'And I am likely to tell you?'

'Probably not.'

'So why are you here?'

'Just say it's a courtesy call.' Ventnor smiled. 'We're tracing the gang. You remember them ... Animal, Soldier, Camel, Coffin Dodger ... I can't remember all their names but we'll trace them.'

'Twenty years is a long time ... people change. It only needs one to have developed a pang of conscience and who was not so close to the murder to be charged with it, but close enough to know who did it and for him to tell us.'

'So...' Webster stood. 'Good luck at your parole hearing ... but that doesn't mean you'll be getting out of gaol.'

Ventnor also stood. 'If we can link you to this murder, you won't be going anywhere, unless it's back to Cat A.'

Hawson paled. 'The nails...?' he pleaded.

Webster patted his jacket pocket. 'I'll hang on to them, we didn't get enough co-operation.'

Driving away from the new low-rise building that is HM Prison, Full Sutton, Ventnor said, 'He'll start making contact.'

'Yes.' Webster smiled. 'We just put a kestrel among the pigeons ... they'll start flapping now. He'll be in touch with whoever he can be.'

'You have to sleep with each member of the gang and then you get taken to a remote location where the biker chicks beat you up and tear off your clothes, leaving you to make your own way home.'

Janet Middleton was a soberly dressed woman in her early forties. Her home was a modest but comfortably furnished semi-detached house in Clifton. Photographs of two children in school uniform stood on the mantelpiece. An elderly border collie that had barked at Hennessey and Yellich until he was calmed, lay curled up at Janet Middleton's feet. 'I'm pleased those days are behind me. I am not ashamed of what I did ... only towards the end ... I just thought differently ... had different values. I'd be horrified today if my daughter went out with a biker. I'd forbid it ... so would my husband. I am very lucky; I made a good marriage to a man who has allowed me to put my past behind me. Not just the biker chick stuff but the offences.'

'Yes, we did have difficulty tracing you, we confess.' Hennessey smiled. 'No convictions for twenty years and even they were petty – shoplifting...'

'Yes, I turned the corner many years ago. I'd be mortified if my children found out I was a criminal.'

'Well ... used to be.'

'Still am, my fingerprints are on file. I have to declare my convictions on any job application form, can't get a visa to visit the States or Australia ... or any place that requires a visa ... got to be clean as the driven snow for that. So my life is well eclipsed.'

'Are you employed?'

'No, I am a housewife. I have had employment ... secretarial work for small businesses ... nothing remarkable. My husband is a public servant, works for the local authority. Money isn't brilliant but he has security of employment and an inflation-proof pension at the end of it all. So things could be worse. I am happy as Mrs Bayfield. Janet Middleton is behind me.'

'Turned a corner as you say ... well done.'

'Thank you.' She paused. 'I read about Terry North. That's what you are here about?'

'Yes. We couldn't tell your parents but we did say that you were not in any trouble.'

'Yes ... they phoned.' She indicated an old-fashioned, ring dial, red phone by the side of the chair. Hennessey thought it an odd place for the only phone in the house, having only ever encountered phones in the living rooms of invalid persons who were chair bound. Nowadays most people had cordless phones they could carry around the house with them. 'They're elderly now ... mid-sixties ... not as elderly as they could be but they are beginning to get easily agitated.'

'It was your last known address, we had to call there.'

'Understand that. I'll phone them later ... let them know I haven't been arrested.'

'So, Terry ... what do you know of him? What do you know of his murder?'

'Not much and nothing, in that order. I remember Terry ... not a major player in the gang ... he and his girlfriend. She was murdered by Harry the Horse, then Terry disappeared ... but I'd gone by then. In fact I was made to ride out for my good hiding on the pillion of Terry North's bike. I felt sick all the way.'

'I can imagine.'

'Well, after it was over, they rode away leaving me to pick myself up ... with my clothes all shredded. Took me five hours to get home – luckily it was high summer ... I waited till dark and then made my way across the fields. Believe me, those Muslim women, the way they have to keep themselves covered up, can't go out of doors unless it's with their husband or mother-in-law ... that ... that is heaven compared to what a biker chick lets herself in for. There's no initiation for a girl but once in, you get bought and sold among the guys and you have no say in it and leaving is fraught, but I went through it just to leave. I mean, ten cigarettes ... I still think I was worth twenty...' She smiled. 'At least twenty.'

Hennessey and Yellich laughed. They both appreciated her humour.

'But that was the last time I saw Terry North ... and his girlfriend was still alive. I remember she wanted to be part of the gang that worked me over, but Animal and the Dungeon Master said "no", they wanted me to ride out there with Terry ... I think Mandy wanted to show Terry what a tough little street fighter she could be.'

'I see ... so the boys watched the spectacle?'

'Oh, yes ... it started when Dungeon Master said "go" and stopped when he said "stop". He let it go on for about fifteen minutes ... that's long enough if twenty chicks are kicking and scratching and punching you.'

'I see. So you had nothing to do with Mandy Fryston's murder? No knowledge of it?'

'Only what I read in the papers and heard on the news. I was all ears because I had known her and I remember Harry the Horse ... that laugh ... bit soft for a biker I always thought so it came as a surprise to hear that he had been done for murder. That wasn't Harry's style. Not only that but Harry and Mandy never had anything between them, they were in the same gang but they never spent any time together and never quarrelled. When you get a group of twenty people, they will split up into sub groups ... Harry and Mandy were just not part of the same group.'

'How long were you a Dungeon chick?'

'About ... about ... little less than two years.'

'Always Animal's girl?'

'Yes ... he introduced me ... and it was fun. At first. Then I saw how the girls get traded for a few cigarettes, a pint of beer, sometimes just given away. Then I found out what happened to girls who wanted to leave ... even took part in that a couple of times myself.'

'You did?'

Janet Bayfield nodded. 'I was between a

rock and a hard place. You know I really understood those Nazis who said, "It was my orders" ... so I did it ... not as hard as I could, but just enough to avoid getting beaten up myself for refusing.'

'Tough life.'

'For the chicks. The boys have the fun ... but the end came when Animal sold me to Camel. He was as loathsome an individual as you could imagine ... and him, you know, he's got convictions for everything.'

'What's his name?' Yellich took out his notepad.

'Smithson ... Shane Smithson ... overweight, never washed and he took pride in that ... treated his women like punch bags ... took pride in that too. Believe me, getting beaten up by the biker chicks after sleeping with each of the gang was a much easier option ... much softer option than becoming Camel's pillion. I did the sensible thing. Believe me ... if the same option was presented tomorrow, I'd make the same decision.'

'So, where was Animal in the hierarchy?'

'Second in command.' She spoke with a clear certainty. 'When the Kings rode out two-by-two, the same six were always in the lead. There was the Dungeon Master, who was always on the outside ... inside of him was Animal ... always those two in front. Then behind them in any order, any position were Soldier, Ranker, the Mad Accountant and Camel ... then there were the middle riders ... like Harry the Horse, the Beast ... Coffin Dodger ... and right at the back was Terry North and Spud.'

'I see.' Hennessey nodded.

'Terry was seen as a bit of a joke because he lived with his parents. Everyone else had their own drum but Terry lived with his parents ... bit sad if you're a biker. Spud was a bit silly but even he had his own place.'

'Even he?'

'He couldn't read or write ... had gone to a special needs school ... inside his head he was about twelve years old.'

Yellich winced inwardly.

'So what was Animal's name?'

'Zielinski, Stefan Zielinski. He was as Yorkshire as they come ... his grandfather had been a Polish Displaced Person. His family kept the Polish culture alive ... big in the Polish community in York ... never

Anglicized the name, used Polish Christian names, but Animal ... strong Yorkshire accent ... all the thee's and thou's ... no h's. "Is this thy 'atchet?" ... that was Animal.'

'How did he get his name?'

'He was a hard man ... a very hard man. He was the Master's enforcer ... the gang feared Animal.'

'So, if Dickie Hawson...' Hennessey saw the look of surprise cross Janet Bayfield's face. 'Oh yes, we know his name, he's inside at the moment.'

'Doesn't surprise me.'

'So, if Hawson wanted someone hurt?'

'Animal would do it. Camel, Soldier and Ranker might be asked to help depending on the job.'

'And Hawson, the Master?'

'He wouldn't get his hands dirty. So while I am not particularly surprised to hear that he is inside ... I am also equally surprised to hear it. Not surprised that he's doing crime, surprised he got caught. He must be losing his touch.'

'What about those days? Was crime done by the gang?'

'I believe so but being a chick, I wasn't

privy to the wheeling and the dealing and the duckin' and divin' and bobbin' and weavin' ... but being Animal's chick my ear was closer to the ground than most of the other chicks ... probably as close as Gaol Bait.'

'Those names...' Once again, Yellich reached for his pad.

'Who was she?' Hennessey asked.

'The Master's chick ... so called because she was under age.'

'How under?'

'Fourteen ... but she was a mature fourteen ... could have passed for seventeen so the Dungeon Master got away with it. Her name was Felicity Appleyard ... lovely name for a very hard girl.'

'So we'll know her?'

'Oh, yes ... much heavier stuff than my shoplifting stupidity. She'll know more about the crime than I would.'

'What do you know?'

'Know? I know nothing ... I can give no statement. I can't speak to anything ... all I can tell you is the rumours ... the whispers.'

'Good enough.'

'Well, Felicity told me that the Master was

getting into a good way of business ... he was talking to people ... serious people. "We won't be getting our hands dirty," she said ... but by "we" I am not sure to whom she was referring, whether "we" being the Dungeon Kings or "we" being the Dungeon Master and her little self. I rather think the latter.'

'What sort of business, did she say?'

'She didn't elaborate but she indicated that the Kings would be carrying stuff ... like Hawson was hiring out the gang as despatch riders ... but carrying what I don't know. Whatever motorbikes are built for, they are not for carrying bulk freight, so whatever it was, it had to be packages.'

'Like controlled substances?'

Janet Bayfield nodded. 'That would be my guess. When I was a chick there was nothing more than the odd joint of cannabis being passed round. So I was thinking he was getting into the hard drug business ... heroin ... in those days it would be heroin ... crack cocaine was being talked about but hadn't really taken off.'

'Yes, I remember.'

'But, as to details ... well, I was a chick,

remember, chicks don't think or do … chicks are just there … nothing else.'

'You sound angry.'

'I am, but with myself in the main, allowing myself to get treated like that. After a while I got used to it … but being sold like that to such a repulsive creature as Camel, that made me see sense even if I had to go through the ordeal of leaving.'

'You couldn't just leave? Just not turn up?'

Janet Bayfield shuddered. 'No … I wouldn't've been able to leave my house … they'd've hounded me, attacked me in the street, slashed my face … I'd've had to leave York. I don't want to live anywhere else … so I had to go through it but they kept their part of the deal, once I had gone through it they left me alone. We'd catch sight of each other from time to time, they didn't acknowledge me and I didn't acknowledge them.'

'I see … so we really need to talk to the lieutenants?'

'Yes … the chicks would not be able to help you.' She smiled. 'Chicks … I say … will you listen to me … chicks … they'll be in their middle years now telling their children to sit up straight in their chairs and pushing them for good results at school. Chicks!'

'Yes ... age comes to us all,' said Hennessey as stories of motorcycles began to reach him on a very personal level, 'if we live long enough.'

'Yes, better than dying young ... and the bikers had an unenviable casualty rate ... not just the Kings but all bikers. Coffin Dodger for one ... he didn't live up to his name.'

'No?'

'No ... he earned his nickname because, even for a biker he was a wild rider ... but he had an early death ... so I heard. After I left, years after, I met another chick who'd also left ... she told me he took a tight bend, a blind corner, at ninety miles an hour and impacted with the back of a petrol tanker that had broken down ... Coffin Dodger took the second prize.'

'As he would.' Hennessey paused. 'The lieutenants?'

'Yes?'

'Animal, Soldier, Ranker, Camel ... they seem to be much of a muchness ... but the Mad Accountant, by his name he seems to stand out. Tell me about him.'

'He did stand out. He was an accountant. He lived a double life. The other guys, apart from a guy called Anglis who worked at his father's pub ... the other guys slept late, dozed around, did a bit of crookin' ... a few dead-end jobs that they didn't or couldn't hold down ... but Bannister was a real live accountant. Got up early, washed shaved, went to work in a suit, came home, climbed into his leathers and got on his 750cc and became a different person. He came from a privileged background, private school, parents both accountants, but he was hard and heavy and reckless enough to be a Dungeon King. I don't know why but the Dungeon Master, Hawson ... Dickie Hawson ... he took a shine to Bannister, the Mad Accountant ... just happens sometimes ... similar to love at first sight between a man and a woman ... two people of the same sex have an instant attraction from the moment they first meet but not in a sexual way. I think it was like that between the Dungeon Master and the Mad Accountant and he was elevated to the inner circle, but he still had to do his seventy-four, still had to ride in close company, still had to keep his end up when the Kings got into a rumble with another gang.'

'What was he like in the gang?'

'Well, he had protection because the Master liked him. He earned respect from the other bikers, but that took a bit of time. He was from a different background, you see ... it was a barrier to full acceptance but he made it ... eventually.'

'Did he have a job? I mean, was he an enforcer for example?'

'The Mad Accountant? Not at all ... he wasn't hard enough, he had brains and perhaps that's what he gave to the gang ... balanced out all the brawn.' She paused. 'Felicity Appleyard would be the one to talk to. The Mad Accountant would call on the Dungeon Master at his drum – his house – they'd talk business. It may be that the Mad Accountant was giving the Master some professional advice about whatever business venture he was setting up.'

Hennessey and Yellich drove back to Micklegate Bar police station. Webster and Ventnor had also returned and were await-ing Hennessey and Yellich.

Hennessey glanced at the clock on the wall of the office shared by Webster and Ventnor and said, 'Right, boys ... late lunch then my office at 14.00 hours ... debrief and see where we go.'

Hennessey observed Webster, Ventnor and Yellich leave the CID corridor to make their way to the canteen, noticing with satisfaction how they formed up into a close group, wanting to be with each other and also how they seemed to fall into step. Pleasingly, he thought, they were gelling as a team. His place, he further thought, his place as team leader meant that he could not gel with them. He had to be a little apart, a little detached.

He left the police station's cool interior and walked into the baking heat of the midday sun and was most grateful for his panama and lightweight suit. He waited until a gap in the traffic afforded a comfortable opportunity to cross the road where he joined the walls, which he took to Lendal Bridge. Moments before he turned to the stairway to climb on to the parapet, his eye was caught by a lone motorcyclist riding noisily up Micklegate who was observing the law by wearing a crash helmet but had otherwise thrown all caution to the wind by wearing only a yellow T-shirt, jeans which had been cut down into shorts, and a pair of sports shoes.

There had, he thought as he climbed the cool stone steps of Micklegate Bar, been far too much of motorcycles that day already for his personal comfort and taste. The morning had been nothing but a dredging up of the first great tragedy of his life. He pondered as he walked the walls, sharing it with many, many others that day, of Graham, his beloved elder brother and his beloved Triumph, of how he would help Graham polish the machine, as it stood outside their parents small terrace house in Greenwich, on Sunday mornings. Of how Graham would then take the young George for a spin up Greenwich Road, into Deptford, across the river by Tower Bridge, past St Paul's, down Ludgate Hill, to Trafalgar Square, then back to the south bank via Westminster Bridge. Good days; golden memories.

Tragedy had struck without warning one summer's night. He lay in bed as he listened to Graham kick his machine into life and then drive away as he then listened to the sound of his brother's bike fade as he climbed through the gears. Other details of the night stayed with him, like the drunk ambling up Colomb Street reciting his Hail Mary's, even the programme his parents were watching on television when there came a knock on the door, the classic police officer's knock: tap, tap ... tap ... The silence, his mother's sudden wailing which went on and on and on, his father's groan, then his father coming to his room, telling him that Graham had ridden his bike to heaven, 'to save a place for us'. Graham had, the police thought, skidded on a patch of oil; certainly no other road user was involved. All George Hennessey's life from that point on had contained a gap where his elder brother should have been and he often wondered what would have become of him.

At the time he died, he had upset and worried their parents, having announced his intention to give up his job in the bank to go to Art College to specialize in photography as the first step to becoming a photographer ... and what a great photographer George

Hennessey believed his brother would have made. Not for him would have been the sleaze and the glamour of fashion photography but the gritty, risky, world of photo journalism, of covering wars and disasters, that would have been Graham Hennessey, who by now would have been a parent, grandparent, and uncle to Charles Hennessey. All that never happened because of a patch of oil on a road in South London one summer's night many years ago, but the memory of which remained fresh. The funeral too was wrong, all wrong, so wrong, not only because it shouldn't have been happening at all, but it was a summer funeral, with the flowers in full bloom, with butterflies flitting by, with birdsong, and instead of sombre music, the coffin was lowered to the sound of merry jingles of ice cream vans which wafted over the grass and the headstones from adjacent streets. Wrong, all wrong. There was, he had always thought after that, something impossibly incongruous about the ceremony of the hole and the stone when it is held in the summer months.

Leaving the walls, he walked across Lendal Bridge which was, as normal, a bottleneck for both road and foot passenger traffic, arching over the Ouse, that was again a pleasant shade of blue and carrying many open top boats catering for tourists. He dined at The York Buttery and, leaving the restaurant feeling fully satisfied, glanced up in awe and wonderment at the Minster and then began a slow stroll back to Micklegate Bar police station, focussing his mind as his lunch settled.

It was Wednesday, the nineteenth of June, 13.40 hours.

Five

Wednesday, 19 June, 14.05 hours – 22.40 hours
*in which useful information is obtained from an
apostate and George Hennessey is at home to
the gracious reader.*

'So...' Hennessey cradled his mug of tea in
his hands and leaned back in his chair,
causing it to creak. 'Where are we ... two
and a half days into the investigation into
the murder of Terence "Terry" North of this
fair city? What's the state of play? Yellich?'
  'Sir?'
'Would you like to recap for us?'
'Well, sir...' Yellich leaned forward. He also
had a mug of tea cradled in his hands,
Webster and Ventnor sat either side of him,
equally imbibing. 'The deceased was a
member of a motorcycle gang which has
now dispersed. Age wearied them and

matured them, one or two are no longer with us, but it appears that the principal gang members are alive and well. They, being the leader of the gang, Richard Hawson, who is presently in Full Sutton and close to being released. The other principal members being Shane Smithson a.k.a. Camel, and one John Bannister a.k.a. the Mad Accountant, Stefan Zielinski a.k.a. the Animal, and two others still known only by their military sounding nicknames of Soldier and Ranker. No one we have talked to has so far admitted any knowledge of the murder of Terry North. We have interviewed Harry the Horse Turner who is out of prison on licence, having admitted his guilt of the murder of Amanda "Mandy" Fryston, but claiming this was only in order to secure an early release. In private he maintains his innocence and seemed very keen to help when he found out we might be looking again at the Mandy Fryston murder. Mandy Fryston and Terry North were an item and they disappeared in close proximity to each other, being three weeks apart. Her body was not concealed and was found quickly; his body was concealed and was only found on Monday last, twenty years after he disappeared following a tip-off from a dying man who had a twinge of conscience. A package containing a suspicious substance was found in Terry North's bedroom by Thompson Ventnor –' Yellich indicated to his right – 'and was sent to Wetherby for analysis. The results will be back any time but it will most likely be a controlled substance.'

'Why do you say that?'

'Because of what Janet Bayfield told us, sir.'

'Which was, for the benefit of Webster and Ventnor who were elsewhere this forenoon...'

'O–of course,' Yellich stammered. 'Sorry. There was an indication that the Dungeon Master was hiring out his crew to work as couriers, not getting involved with the importation or the distribution, but conveying it from the importer at the docks or the airport to the distributor in York. Dangerous work but only if you are caught by the law. Not part of the high risk of getting it through customs, nor the messy end of selling it in small packages ... the neat part, and he tended to use those low down in the hierarchy to do the work, those that hung on and were hungry for acceptance ... and not likely to inform on him.'

'OK ... anything to add? Ventnor, Webster?'

'We visited Hawson in Full Sutton this forenoon.'

'Did you?'

'Yes, sir, following on from our visiting Nicholas Sitwell ... one time member of the Dungeon Kings, now a driver of pensioners on coach trips to the coastal resorts. It seemed a logical extension to call in on Hawson.'

'Yes ... wouldn't have done any harm but rather you had cleared it with me. You do have a mobile phone?'

'Yes, sir.'

'Well, use it, please ... it would have taken all of thirty seconds.'

'Yes, sir.'

'So, what did you find?'

'A tough guy who doesn't like being banged up, very cocky about his early parole, very angry about something ... likely he has a chip on his shoulder. He did not give anything away ... he seemed worried by our investigation though. We felt we had stirred something up which was to our advantage. As Reginald said, "We put a kestrel among the pigeons".'

'So, what's for action?' Hennessey leaned forward, picked up a pen from his desk top, and held it poised over his notepad.

'We're getting a sort of lip service of co-operation, sir,' Webster offered, 'so it seems, a sort of superficial willingness to talk but at a deeper level they are observing the biker code ... not ratting on each other.'

Hennessey nodded. 'Confess I felt the same. All Yellich and I seemed to get is, "I don't know anything but go and talk to so and so."'

'Aye,' Yellich said as he drained his mug, 'pretty soon we'll have interviewed every living member of the gang and not be any the wiser.'

'Yes...' Hennessey drummed his fingers on his desk top. 'So, what do we do?'

'I think we ought to have another look at the Mandy Fryston murder,' Yellich suggested. 'Like every other cop, I'd be very rich if I had a fiver or a tenner for every felon who claimed innocence despite being convicted, but I believed Turner ... in my waters I thought he was telling the truth when he said he had been framed.'

'I will say I came away with my mind also opening to the possibility of a wrongful conviction, though my waters spoke less strongly than yours clearly did, but nonetheless, we will have a look at the murder of Mandy Fryston ... they were an item, she and Terry North.'

'And her brooch was found in his grave, as if tossed in with the body,' Yellich added.

'Yes, by which time Harry the Horse Turner was in custody.'

'If the Dungeon Master is anything to go by,' Webster offered, 'the gang members are still pretty low life. It has been suggested before that the way in is to approach those who have something to lose. If Bannister was an accountant...?'

'He appears to have been.'

'Well, if he was, and if he remained in this area, he'll be in his forties now ... consolidating nicely, he won't want us sniffing round him, asking him questions about a murder. He'll be very pleased to talk ... per-haps.'

'Perhaps ... but it's a fair perhaps.' Hen-nessey made a long arm and picked up the *Yellow Pages* that lay at the corner of his desk. He opened it as the other officers sat in silence. 'Well,' he said at length, 'no chart-ered accountants in York called Bannister, John, so if he is practising he is employed by a firm and has not gone solo. Job for you, Webster ... Find him.'

'Yes, boss.'

'Then chat to him ... just take the measure of him in the first instance ... work with Ventnor.'

'Yes, sir. The other guy I was thinking of is the publican's son.'

'Anglis?'

'Yes, sir ... now a publican in his own right.'

'Yes.'

'Son-in-law of Robert Prendergahst MP, no less.'

'Minister for Trade and Industry,' Hen-nessey said with a smile. 'Yes, he won't want publicity, not with an election looming that his father-in-law's party needs to win if he is going to keep his Cabinet office. Yes, I am sure he'll be very co-operative ... call back on him.'

'Yes, sir.'

'Yellich and I have met him, all too briefly ... but enough to worry him. You and I, Yellich, we'll dig out the file on Mandy Fryston ... look at it with a fresh eye ... a fresh pair of eyes. I also think Harry Turner merits a re-visit.'

Hennessey and Yellich stepped out of the car and nodded to Harry the Horse Turner who sat in a reclining chair outside his small cottage. The garden smelled sweetly of freshly turned soil as the two officers strode calmly up the path to the building.

'Back so soon?' Harry Turner stood as they approached.

'Yes, as you see –' Hennessey stepped up onto the front porch – 'enquires continue apace but we thought we would pick your brains before we made our next call.'

'Your next call?'

'Well, among other things, we will be taking a fresh look at the murder of Mandy Fryston.'

'Thank you, I appreciate that.'

'Well, it is in your interest if what you have told us is true, but to be honest you are not our primary concern.'

'No?'

'No.' Hennessey shook his head.

'The primary concern is to serve the ends of justice. Two murders have been committed, they have to be investigated. If, in the course of the investigation, it transpires that a man was wrongfully convicted, then that is another issue. It might be hugely significant to you ... but it's still another issue.'

'OK ... so how can I help?'

'We need advice.'

'Oh ... shall we go inside? I can't be seen talking to you ... I think I am being watched.'

'Really?'

'Yes, really.' Harry Turner opened his door and invited the officers to enter.

'Not working on the garden today?' Hennessey remarked as he entered the cottage. 'I see no tools.'

'Too humid ... too close. I mean, look, visibility is down to ... what would you say? A mile? Total cloud cover, yet it's like an oven.

Your body can't sweat properly. On a day like today it would be dangerous to exert yourself.'

'Sensible.' Hennessey stepped into Turner's cottage, which on that day was no cooler within than was the air temperature without. 'Watched, you say?'

'Well ... take a seat.' Turner folded himself into an armchair as the officers each also sat in vacant chairs.

'Yes, the road is quiet, not a lot of traffic but last night, a bike went past a few times ... six times ... sounded like the same machine. Rode up slowly and then when it was bang outside my cottage, it accelerated away. Watched is the wrong word ... I'm being ... *threatened* ... that's the right word.'

'Intimidated.' Hennessey sat back in the chair. 'You are being intimidated ... and that is interesting.'

'Yes, it's an old biker trick. I used to do it.'

'You did?'

'Yes. I am not proud of it but if someone was beginning to stray ... if someone might be going to talk to the law, then we'd do that. Ride up slowly then accelerate when right opposite their house. Did it a few times during the course of one night, usually had the wanted effect.'

'So someone doesn't want you to talk to us?'

'Seems so.'

'Who would the rider be?'

'Someone from the Dungeon Kings. They might not be a biker gang anymore but they will still have their bikes. It never leaves you. You might not have such a powerful machine ... might not ride as fast, but you still need the thrill of the ride. More sense of movement than you get in a car ... so they'll have their bikes still ... kept out of sight in many cases but they'll be there. They won't contract out to a younger team ... they keep their own house.'

'We are learning more and more about the biker code ... keeping their own house in order, that's another new piece of information. If you are being intimidated it helps us, narrows the field down. What time did this happen?' asked Hennessey.

'About one a.m., between one and half one.'

'Did you look out?'

'No ... I didn't...' Turner's voice faltered. 'I

got the message.'

'But you're still talking to us.'

'Yes, I want to clear my name. If I want that, I've got to talk to you. So you want to pick my brains?'

'Two things. We need more information about the transporting of heroin by the Dungeon Kings.'

Turner raised his eyebrows. 'I told you already all I know.'

'Well, we need more details if you want us to help you,' Hennessey explained.

'So, what do you know?' Yellich probed.

'Fair enough ... well Animal and the Dungeon Master set it up. The Dungeon Master was the brains and the driving force. He wanted to be a big-time crim but he was scared of gaol, so he won't be a happy camper right now ... eating all that porridge ... but he wanted into the drug business.'

'Offered the use of the Dungeon Kings as couriers, is that right?'

'Yes.'

'But the low value Kings ... the ones at the bottom of the pecking order?'

'Yes ... just like I told you before.'

'We don't know the extent of it ... the

contacts he collected it from ... who he delivered it to...?'

'And how large an operation it was,'Yellich added, 'and how long did it go on for? If we are going to penetrate the wall of silence, we need more information.'

'The wall of silence?' Turner glanced at Yellich.

'Which is the other thing we want your advice about. We talk to people who were in the Dungeon Kings, they will tell us a little, but only a little, and refer us on to someone else. We need advice about how to get in ... we need an apostate.'

'An apostate?'

'Someone who has renounced his belief, whatever that belief is,' Hennessey explained.

'Which,' added Yellich, 'which, in this case, is the biker's code.'

Turner settled back in his chair and closed his eyes. 'So, I suppose that's me ... I have to be an apostate.' He opened them again. 'I can't give evidence in court.'

Hennessey paused. 'Why not?' He held eye contact with Turner. 'I mean, you are not in the gang anymore because the gang no longer exists ... and the gang that did exist may or may not have set you up to take the blame for the murder of Mandy Fryston ... There's nothing to be loyal to.'

'There isn't, is there?' Turner spoke softly. 'Since you put it like that.'

'That's the only way to put it,' Hennessey said firmly. 'So, can you help us and help yourself?'

'I'll have to be careful.' He pointed to the window. 'They won't be satisfied with putting me in hospital ... it will be worse than that.'

'Do you need protection?'

Turner shook his head. 'I don't know ... I have one of these.' He took a mobile phone from his pocket. 'In future we should talk on the phone. I can use this from inside here, and it's a pay-as-you-go mobile so no one can trace my calls.'

'Good idea. You have our office number, we can give you our own mobile numbers also ... phone or text any time.'

'OK.'

'So what can you tell us?'

'Well, you are right about the transportation of heroin. It went on for about six months and at its height, involved most of the gang, not just the likes of Terry North and Mandy Fryston and the other hangers-on.'

'Including yourself?'

'Yes,' Turner said as he nodded his head. 'I made a couple of short runs.'

'Short runs?'

'Hull to York. It was fairly low risk for us so the money wasn't great.'

'You would have collected a very long gaol sentence if caught in possession of heroin with intent to sell. That's not a great risk?'

'Not in comparison to the risk of being caught smuggling it through customs ... not in comparison to the risk you take distributing it. I was in possession of it for just over half an hour, being the time it took to travel from Hull to York. Nice steady ride, did nothing to attract the attention of the traffic cops. I looked like a motorcycle enthusiast rather than a biker. And I was fitted with a quick release gear.'

Turner held up his right hand. 'This. I carried my brick inside my jacket ... had a deep pocket inside my jacket ... if I was rumbled I would drive into a country lane and when I was out of sight of any following police car or bike I would pull it out of the pocket and chuck it away. The customers didn't like that ... wanted me to carry it in the pannier ... reckoned it was safer. I won't be admitting to this, by the way, this is off the record. Even though there are two of you this isn't a taped interview and I won't be signing any confession. I've been inside, I don't want to go back, even if it was for some crime I did do.'

'OK,' Hennessey said, 'we are after bigger fish than someone who transported heroin twenty years ago. We have to win some and to lose some, but if someone was to give information against you and had proof ... let's just say, it's a risk you take.'

Turner's eyes narrowed. He fixed Hennessey with an icy stare, then he stood and walked to the window and looked out over his small garden to the road and the fields and woodlands that lay beyond the road. 'I'm putting my life on the line for you and you still prosecute me?' He turned to Hennessey. 'What am I helping you for in that case?'

'Well, you want to clear your name in

174

respect of the Mandy Fryston murder.'

'Yes ... but not if it means another stretch inside ... for something I did twenty years ago.'

'Well, it's up to you.' Hennessey stood. 'The best thing you can do is put your information on the record in return for immunity from prosecution ... but that's got to be on the record. Then I'd think about witness protection if I were you.'

'I can't be seen to go willingly ... these fields have eyes.'

'And the woods have ears. We can help you there. Mr Yellich?'

Yellich stood and withdrew a pair of handcuffs from his jacket pocket.

Thompson Ventnor thought that John Bannister looked worried.

Very worried.

'I–I can't offer you a great deal of time,' Bannister stammered apologetically. 'We ... I have a client ... a very important client coming in ten minutes, I can't keep him waiting.' He was smartly dressed in a dark suit. Slim build.

'No matter ... so long as we know where to

find you,' Ventnor said with a smile, but he allowed menace to show in his eyes.

'How did you find me?'

'*Yellow Pages*,' Webster replied, also with a smile. 'Just phoned all the accountancy firms in York asking to speak to Mr John Bannister. The response we usually got was, "No, sorry, no one of that name works here", until the tenth or eleventh call when a sweet-voiced receptionist said, "Who shall I say is calling?" So we just said, "Thanks, we'll call round" ... so here we are at Adams and Co.'

'That was you? Oh, Erica told me about that call, I've been wondering who it could have been.'

'Now you know.' Thompson Ventnor scanned Bannister's office: small, cramped, a desk piled high with folders and files on which also stood the framed photograph of a dark-haired young woman. The small window behind him looked out on to the Ouse and the roofline of Old York. The building itself, he thought, was mid-Victorian. A modern clock, with a white clock face of Roman numerals and an audible tick, was mounted on the wall to Bannister's left, spider plants sat on the windowsill; on the wall opposite the clock was a print of Rembrandt's *Man in Armour*. The room smelled of carpet freshener. Air conditioning kept the room pleasantly cool.

'So, how can I help you?' He glanced at the clock. 'In the eight minutes I have to spare.'

'Not much in that case, we'll have to call back.'

'Alright, but in respect of what?'

'Murder.' Webster spoke softly and as he did so, he enjoyed watching the colour drain from Bannister's face.

'Murder?'

'Yes, of a girl called Mandy or Amanda Fryston. You might remember her from the days of your youth. You are the John Bannister a.k.a. the Mad Accountant who did his seventy-four to join the Dungeon Kings … this being about twenty years ago?'

Colour continued to drain from Bannister's face. He sank back in his chair.

'You remember those days? The bikers and biker chicks you rode with? Master, Animal, Soldier, Ranker?' Webster prompted.

'Camel, Harry the Horse, Coffin Dodger ... Andy Anglis...' added Ventnor. 'We've been tracking them all down ... those that are still alive. Coffin Dodger is no longer dodging his coffin ... you may or may not know.'

'Oh ... what happened?'

'Biking accident ... inevitable, really, given his riding style ... so we hear. So, we are talking to the right man?'

'Yes ... I was a biker, an act of rebellion against a middle-class background. A friend of mine joined the army as a private soldier for the same reason.'

'So long as we have the right person. We are investigating the murder of Terry North. You remember Terry? A bit of a hanger-on ... not a powerful member of the gang?'

'Yes ... Terry ... he did his seventy-four though, otherwise he wouldn't have been in.'

'Yes, but when you went out in a group he always rode near the back?'

'Yes, he was a back rider.'

'You were up near the front?'

'Yes. We rode two abreast, the Dungeon Master and Animal were always in the front, then Soldier and Ranker, then me and Camel ... driving out somewhere ... for a pint at the Three Cranes at Stamford Bridge, or a run out to the coast.'

'We've contacted a few of the gang, like Nicholas Sitwell, then known as the Mad Builder.'

'Ah, yes.' Bannister smiled. 'How is he?'

'Settled in middle years as a coach driver.'

'A coach driver! Well, well...'

'Well, we have only a few minutes, we won't keep you if you have an important client.'

'Appreciated.'

'We need to get closer to the inner circle. What was Ranker's real name?'

'Ranker? I remember him, of course...'

'Yes, his name?'

'I only ever knew him as Ranker ... this *was* twenty years ago.'

'Soldier?'

'Again ... I only knew him as Soldier.'

'Why was he called Soldier?'

'He was one ... a soldier, I mean ... assaulted an officer, got some time in military custody, then a dishonourable discharge.'

'I see. So, if you do remember their real

names...'

Bannister shrugged, 'If they come to me.'

'Well, this is off the record. If we caution you and if under caution you still deny knowing their names and we subsequently find out that you do know them, we will be charging you with obstruction.' Ventnor spoke firmly.

'This is a murder investigation,' Webster reminded him. 'In fact it may be a double murder.'

'Double?' Bannister's voice cracked.

'Yes, we are looking again at the murder of Mandy Fryston.'

'Mandy Fryston? Harry the Horse went down for that.'

'Well, he's come back up again, claiming wrongful conviction and we ... well, we are prepared to take another look at the murder.'

'They're linked, you see,' Ventnor said with a smile. 'Terry North was murdered in his biker gear ... battered to death ... and Mandy Fryston's gold brooch was found in his grave, not in one of his pockets but underneath his body.'

'The hole was dug, the brooch thrown in,

and his body thrown on top of the brooch,' Webster explained.

'But Harry the Horse was in custody by the time Terry was murdered,' Ventnor added. 'Hence our curiosity, hence our willingness to open our minds to Harry Turner's claim that he was wrongfully convicted.'

The phone on Bannister's desk warbled. He picked it up and said, 'Yes ... thank you ... ask him to take a seat.' He replaced the phone. 'That's my client,' he said with a weak voice. 'I'll have to see him directly.'

'We'll call back, or shall we call you at home?'

'At home might be better.' He took his wallet from his jacket. 'That's my business card, it has my home phone number as well as my business number.' He handed the card to Ventnor.

'Thank you.' Ventnor put it in his pocket.

'The home number is ex-directory but I know the police can access ex-directory addresses.' There was a note of agitation in his voice. 'I live alone ... I don't go out much. If you don't mind late working or weekend working?'

'We don't at all.' Ventnor stood.

181

'Oh...' Webster also stood. 'We know about the transportation of heroin, so anything you remember would be in your interest to tell us.'

Bannister's jaw sagged.

'Can't say it's all coming back to me –' Harry the Horse Turner drew on the cigarette – 'it never really went away. A few details maybe, but the main things are still in here.' He tapped the side of his head.

'So, in your own words...' Hennessey prompted.

'Immunity from prosecution is agreed?' The short and slightly built man who had given his name as Julian Parkes, of Ellis, Burden, Woodland and Lake, solicitors, glanced at Hennessey.

'Yes, it is,' Hennessey said as he nodded, 'unless your client confesses to an exceptionally serious crime.'

'That's too imprecise.' Parkes was smartly dressed. Hennessey thought him 'dapper', in a word.

'We could not turn a blind eye to murder or arson or similar.'

'It's alright...' Turner took another drag on

the cigarette. 'Nothing like that.'

'And I will advise your client if he is getting into dangerous ground.'

'Very well.' Parkes sat back but kept his pen poised over his notepad.

'Well, the heroin run ... picked it up from Hull and also London.'

'Specific addresses?'

'I never did the London run, but the Hull run, that was from an address in East Hull, an ordinary terraced house, 123 April Avenue. The place was a staging post. How it got from Hull docks to the house, I don't know. I just went to the door, asked for Big Tim ... said, "Dick sent me"...'

'Richard Hawson, the Dungeon Master?'

'Yes.'

Hennessey and Yellich glanced at each other and raised their eyebrows. 'He won't be getting out as soon as he thinks,' Hennessey growled. 'So then what?'

'I drove it to York and handed it to Tony Wells, usually Tony, sometimes to Stefan ... also known as Animal.'

'Any witnesses to this?'

'No witnesses in Hull, but in York ... yes ... the gang was there ... not all of them. I only ever did four runs.'

'Who did Tony Wells deliver it to?'

'He didn't. Some fella collected it. Fella called, the Turk.'

'The Turk?' Hennessey repeated.

'Appearance?' Yellich asked.

'Late twenties, clean shaven, strongly built ... never went anywhere without his minders, three men in a flash car ... a Jaguar ... 771 WJ.'

'That was the registration?'

'Yes ... remembered it because my bike was 771 WG. It's the sort of thing I notice ... and remember.'

Hennessey wrote the registration number on his pad.

'It's still in York, I've seen it ... it's a classic car. Don't know who owns it. The guy at the wheel wasn't the Turk. The Turk must have sold it on and it was eventually bought by an enthusiast who didn't know it had been tainted with drug money during its life.'

'If it's still in existence, we can trace the Turk. DVLA of Swansea keeps computerized records of all existing cars and their previous owners. This is good, Harry, we won't be prosecuting you for carrying the heroin, not in exchange for this information. See how it works? You scratch our back...' Hennessey paused. 'Now ... the murder of Terry North, tell us about that.'

'Well, I'll tell you what I know. Terry and his chick, Mandy, they were regular couriers; they could be sacrificed unto the law. The Dungeon Master could afford to do without them so they did a lot of runs ... him and the other lower ranking members like Coffin Dodger and Beast. Anyway, the way I heard it was that Mandy got greedy.'

'Oh no!' Hennessey put his hand to his head. 'She didn't steal a brick?'

'Right, first time. That caused serious problems for the Dungeon Master, he had to pay the value of it to the Turk. A brick of uncut heroin ... street value of a million pounds. The Turk would have paid Big Tim in Hull say ... one hundred thousand, possibly more ... I don't know the figure ... Then it was the Turk who paid Dick Hawson, say a thousand, for the carrying of it ... which Hawson split between him and the courier.'

'Nice earner for the Dungeon Master.'

'Very nice. Not doing anything for five

hundred a week and that was twenty years ago when five hundred was worth five hundred.'

'There were weekly runs?'

'Near as damn it.'

'So, Mandy got light-fingered?'

'Yes … she and Terry were shifting a brick and came back to York saying they'd lost it.'

'A likely story.'

'That's what the Dungeon Master thought. She wouldn't say what'd happened to it … it was round that time that she and then Terry went missing. Her body was found. His wasn't until a few days ago. Anyway, I was visited when I was in prison awaiting trial by Andrew Anglis, him and me used to partner up when the gang rode out … we were mates. Anyway, Andrew told me that the Master had to pay the Turk the value of the brick and that would not have been cheap … but what hurt the Master was that his street cred went west. The courier business was a toehold for him, the first step into the premier division of organized crime, which is where he wanted to be. After Mandy Fryston half-inched the brick, he was finished … unreliable … it was that which hurt him. He knew he'd never recover and he hasn't, by all accounts he's now just a petty crook ... a nobody. The courier service was going to be the beginning for him, the foundation. Instead it was the high point of his life. No wonder Terry and Mandy disappeared.'

Hennessey shook his head. 'You don't mess with people like that. They should have known that...'

'Terry would have, but Mandy...' Turner opened the palm of his left hand as he dogged the nail with his right. 'She was a very pushy girl, especially for a biker chick. Bikers like their chicks meek and obedient, which she was most of the time, but when she was with Terry, she was the boss and she would have convinced him they could get away with it. I'm surprised they went back to York with the cock-and-bull story about losing it ... if they had just kept riding ... but they didn't.'

'OK ... so if ... if ... you were fitted up for Mandy Fryston's murder...'

'I was.'

'For now it's "if".' Hennessey spoke softly but firmly. 'If you were fitted up for her murder, why you? You seem to have been middle-ranking in the gang, someone whom Richard Hawson valued. Did he have it in for you for something? Had you quarrelled, perhaps?'

Turner leaned back in his chair. 'You know, come to think of it, I did have a set to with Animal.'

'Stefan Zielinski?'

'Stefan? Yes. Not serious, never came to blows ... just a flare up ... but that might have been enough. Have a fight with Animal and you have a fight with the Dungeon Master ... and vice versa. They were tight, those two ... I mean, really tight.'

'They may still be.' Hennessey glanced at Yellich. 'Haven't had the pleasure of meeting Zielinski yet have we, Yellich?'

'Not yet, sir ... not yet, but I do think we ought to make his acquaintance.'

'So do I.' Hennessey then turned to Turner. 'Two names keep cropping up ... Soldier and Ranker ... tell us of them.'

'Enforcers, always rode behind Animal and the Dungeon Master but ahead of everyone else ... they were the first lieutenants of the gang.'

'Names?'

'Sorry, I can't ... really ... I am turning Queen's evidence here, I am not going to withhold any information, especially as insignificant as real names. You should look in your box of tricks ... those two had serious form. You'll have them down as a.k.a. Ranker and Soldier.'

Hennessey glanced at Yellich, who looked embarrassed and who then said, 'I'll get on it, sir.' He made to stand.

'Afterwards.' Hennessey laid a hand on Yellich's forearm. 'It can wait.'

'Tell us about the Mad Accountant and Andrew Anglis.'

'Bannister and Anglis ... well ... they were there because the Dungeon Master liked them. They were a bit classy, a bit educated and he liked that ... it appealed to him ... but the rest of the crew were not happy about it, didn't like the posh boys. It was the one thing that Animal and the Dungeon Master argued about ... but the Master got his own way. I mean, he was the Master of the Kings and the Master ruled.'

'So was there ill feeling in the gang? I mean towards Bannister and Anglis?'

'From Animal, Ranker and Soldier ... the rest were not too bothered either way. Bannister and Anglis were OK lads ... good blokes, and that was all that mattered. They'd done the seventy-four and didn't act posh, didn't put on their fancy airs ... so they were OK, but it was as though that wasn't good enough for those three, Animal, Ranker and Soldier, they wanted something more from them ... they wanted them to prove themselves in some way. I think the Mad Accountant was helping the Master with his business, showing him how to launder money ... but I wasn't a part of that, and that wasn't good enough for Animal, Ranker or Soldier, they wanted some display of macho. They wanted testosterone out of Bannister and Anglis ... not bookkeeping.'

'That's interesting. So if Bannister and Anglis didn't come up with the goods, what would have happened to them?'

'They'd get rolled, badly done over. They were annoying Animal and the other two ... They wouldn't be allowed to leave after buying all the beer one night. They were lasses in the eyes of those three and they would have got what the lasses got when they wanted out. They would have woken up in hospital ... if they woke up at all.'

'But they had the Master's protection?'

'Yes. But I think that was wearing thin ... the Master had to balance his protection of them against the possible loss of loyalty from those three. It was about then that I was banged up for some petty crime and didn't get out for a few months.'

'Things for Bannister and Anglis were critical, would you say?'

'Yes ... yes ... I like that word ... critical ... yes, they were critical.'

'And how about you? Do you still want protection?'

'No.' Turner smiled. 'I can handle myself, and their scare tactics don't impress me. I'll be alright,' he assured them, but Hennessey felt there was an edge of fear in his bravado.

Hennessey sat at his desk, recording the content of Turner's interview into the file of the murder of Terence North. He was so absorbed in his task that he didn't notice Commander Sharkey standing in the doorway of his office. Only when Sharkey tapped on the door, did he glance up.

191

'Oh ... sorry, sir.'

'May I?' Sharkey indicated the chairs in front of Hennessey's desk.

'Please do, sir. How can I help you?'

'Sorry to intrude.' Sharkey was small for a police officer and impeccably dressed, so much so that he refused to take off his waistcoat, jacket and tie in concession to the heat, the only air conditioning in the building being the ability to open windows here and there. He slid into a chair. 'Just the old question, George. I am haunted by Johnny Taighe ... our maths teacher at school.'

'He had a massive coronary. I think you have mentioned the tragedy ... yes, sir.'

'I am sure I have. Didn't see it at the time ... how could I? How could we? We were fifteen years old ... but overweight, red face and nose ... smoked like it was going out of fashion. He was a heart attack waiting to happen ... all the signals ... all the warning signs ... even his false good humour. Not one of his colleagues or the headmaster picked it up. Instead they piled on the pressure, just when he should have been allowed to coast to a well-earned retirement, they piled on the pressure. He was good, very good at lower school maths but two years before he could retire with a good pension he was told to teach senior school to national certificate level ... makes me angry when I look back ... George, I don't want to...'

Hennessey held up his hand. 'Sir, we have had this conversation before. I do not want to retire from a desk. I appreciate your concern. I finished my stint in the Navy by walking off a destroyer and I want to finish my days in the force by walking down the CID corridor. I am up to the job. I don't feel under stress ... pressure, yes ... it helps get the job done, but not stress. I sleep at night and get through the days without nicotine and the evenings without alcohol excess. But thank you for your concern. It is appreciated.'

Sharkey, ten years younger than Hennessey, smiled and nodded, 'So long as you are sure, George. I don't want a repeat of that incident in my nick. Just ask if you change your mind. You have put in long years of excellent service. There are openings for senior officers in the Child and Family Unit and the Training Section.'

'I'm happy here, sir.' Hennessey tapped his desk. 'Very happy, deliriously so ... I assure you.'

'Very well.' Sharkey adjusted his position in the chair in which he sat. 'The other thing ... I left the army and joined the Royal Hong Kong Police, as it was.'

'I remember, sir ... seen the photograph on your office wall.'

'Yes ... there as a penance, there as a reminder of sins past ... not there out of pride. You just couldn't escape the corruption in the Royal Hong Kong Police, it was everywhere. Not in the same manner as corruption that occurs in the UK police from time to time. It was a negative corruption, if you like, a sergeant would tell me not to patrol a specific area on a specific night, so I didn't, and an envelope of cash would be in my desk drawer the following morning. It was endemic. I was only there for a few months but I was there and I was part of it, George.'

'I am sure there's no bent coppers in this nick, sir ... sure of it.'

'I am reassured, George.' Sharkey stood. 'I couldn't cope if there was a rotten apple. Anyway, have a good evening.'

194

Hennessey remained in the premises of Micklegate Bar police station addressing clerical matters – tedious but so, so important – until he felt that the homeward bound traffic would have eased sufficiently to allow him a smooth and unhindered drive home. As he approached his house in Easingwold his heart leapt for there, half on and half off the grass verge, was a silver BMW. Ten minutes later, having given attention to Oscar, he and his son sat in wooden chairs on the patio at the rear of his house, sipping tea, whilst Oscar explored the lengthening and welcome shadows in the garden.

'Got a sensible one.' Charles sipped tea from his mug. 'He's as guilty as guilty could be and thank goodness, he's going G.'

'Automatic one third off.' Hennessey watched his dog.

'Yes ... do so hate it when they insist on going N.G. when they are clearly guilty. Just dig themselves in deeper.'

'Yes ... but try telling them that. How are the children?'

'Thriving ... keep wondering when Grand-dad is going to visit again.'

'As soon as he can,' Hennessey said with a

smile. 'Grandchildren are more fun ... you can put them back on the shelf when you have finished with them.'

'Yes ... couldn't have been easy for you bringing me up by yourself.'

'I had help.'

'Yes, but a paid daily isn't the same as a partner ... and speaking of which, when are we going to meet your new friend?'

'Oh ... soon, I think ... quite soon.'

Later, his son departed, Oscar fed and exercised and himself suppered and rested, with the company of a good book George Hennessey strolled into Easingwold. Enjoying the evening and observing the swallows circling at a higher altitude to catch the insects which had been elevated by the uplifting currents of warm air, he then had a pint of Brown and Mild at the Dove Inn, just one, before last orders were called.

It was Wednesday, the nineteenth of June, 22.40 hours.

Six

Thursday, 20 June, 10.15 hours – 13.10 hours
in which pressure is applied and a man decides to go willingly.

Hennessey thought that Somerled Yellich looked pleased with himself. He said so.

'Well –' Yellich raised his eyebrows as he lowered himself into the chair in front of Hennessey's desk – 'appearances are deceptive ... or am I giving the wrong signals? A grimace can be mistaken for a smile.'

'You are not pleased?' Hennessey leaned back in his chair.

'Well, yes and no. I am not pleased that a felon should have told us our job but pleased that we got a result. I entered the two nicknames Ranker and Soldier into our criminal records database as possible a.k.a.'s.'

'As Turner suggested?'

'Yes, sir.'

'Well, he may not be a serious felon after all...'

'Small consolation, sir, we should have done it ourselves ... incomplete check ... but nonetheless we have a result.' He handed Hennessey the computer printout.

'Norbert Soldier Strubby,' Hennessey read, 'care of Strubby's Garage, Frosterly. Where's that?'

Yellich shrugged. 'Came straight here, boss. Be easy enough to locate, though.'

'Yes ... and Philip Ranker Heath, Main Road, Murton. Well, we know where that is, at least, small farming village to the east of York.'

'Yes, sir.'

'Do we visit them now or later? What do you think?'

'Well ... I still think we ought to put pressure on the so-called Mad Accountant and Anglis. We know Ranker and Soldier, they've got form for violence ... they'll be hard nuts to crack, especially as they were lieutenants, second only to the Master and Animal.'

'Still quite high up, though, but I think you are correct, we'd better lean on the vulnerable area. We'll do that. What are Ventnor and Webster doing?'

'Interviewing the parents of Mandy Fryston, sir.'

'That's her.' Sydney Fryston nodded to the photograph on the mantelpiece.

Webster picked it up and looked at it before handing it to Ventnor. It showed a girl who, Ventnor thought, was plain of face, looking straight into the camera. The eyes, he thought, had a steely determination about them. He put the photograph back on the mantelpiece.

'Things were never the same after that man Turner did her in,' Mandy's father continued. 'Our Meg, she just pined and pined and pined. That's her chair...' He nodded to an armchair that was noticeably free of clutter, unlike the table top and settee which held old newspapers, unwashed plates and cutlery; flies buzzed about the room and the bodies of dead flies lay on many surfaces. Thompson Ventnor noticed a can of fly spray wedged between Fryston and the arm of the chair in which he sat and imagined Fryston periodically taking the can and spraying the room without leaving the chair. 'Aye, we was in the house ... here ... Meg kept it lovely ... always so clean, so spick and span, and it was after our Mandy had been murdered ... she couldn't work, the house was getting bad and folk stopped calling round to see us ... and you could smell the house from the street.'

Still can, thought Webster, but his lips remained closed.

'Anyway, we were watching television and I noticed Meg's head had fallen forward and I said, "Are you tired, pet?" I said, "If you're tired we'll go up, it's getting late anyway", but she didn't answer and I said, "Are you alright, lass?" And there was no response ... then I was a widower. She just faded ... bit like our Tom.'

'Tom?'

'My brother. He woke up one morning, winter time it was, rain hammering on the glass and he couldn't understand why his Meg ... we both married women called Margaret, so for years it was Sydney's Meg and Tom's Meg in our family ... anyway, he couldn't understand why his Meg wasn't moving to make his morning cup of tea for him. He reached out and he said she was cold and stiff. She'd gone in her sleep. So, both called Meg, both went before their husbands and both in their sleep ... except our Meg passed in the chair. Wouldn't have liked to wake up next to her like our Tom did his Meg.'

'Sorry to hear that, but we really need to talk about Amanda.'

'Aye ... I think about her every day. What father wouldn't? She'd be middle-aged now ... children. I'd be a granddad; I'd feel like keeping my house clean so my grandchildren would visit. Meg would still be alive, I know she would. So what can I tell you? We didn't like her friends ... those bikers ... those leather jackets, never saw any violence, but it was always there in the background ... that ... sense of it. Never saw a mark on Mandy but overheard her talking to her boyfriend one day, about how they were going to beat up a biker chick who wanted to leave the gang. That was my little girl who played with dolls and had a tea set ... and she grew up. Well, growing up isn't the word ... one day ... suddenly she was a young woman talking about beating up chicks. Our Meg was fair upset about it but you couldn't do anything.'

'Did you meet any of her friends?'

'Only her boyfriend ... Terence ... nice lad ... quiet ... not particularly aggressive in himself, took a fair shine to our Mandy. The rest ... well, just a gang of bikers calling on her.'

'When did you see him last?'

'Last time I saw her, they were together at the door, just the two of them and our Mandy said, "Take it home with you, put it somewhere ... even if it's under your bed". It was after that Mandy first, then Terence a few weeks later, went missing. She was found, he never was. It's a mystery what happened to him ... a real mystery.'

'You don't watch television, Mr Fryston?'

'No –' he glanced at the television in the corner of the room – 'that old thing doesn't work and I don't read the papers ... I've just got no time for the world. Not now. Not with our Mandy and our Meg away. No time for the world at all.'

The two officers left the house and walked

down the path beside the overgrown garden, grateful to be able to breathe clean, summer air. Around them were pleasant houses, well-kept gardens, clean cars in driveways, well-scrubbed children playing on skateboards, and an ice-cream van clearly doing good business.

Hennessey and Yellich walked to the University Arms pub, arriving before it had opened for business. They knocked on the door in which was a glass panel, through which they could see a woman in a smock, who was vacuum-cleaning the floor. She turned at their knock and tapped her watch and mouthed, 'Eleven o'clock, love'. Hennessey and Yellich grinned. Yellich held up his ID. The woman pressed the foot control of the vacuum cleaner and hurried to the door, turned a single lock and opened it. 'Sorry, love...'

'Police.' Yellich smiled.

'Yes?'

'Is Mr Anglis in?'

'I don't think so. I'll get the under manager ... he's in the cellar racking the real ale. Please come in.' She stepped aside and

Hennessey and Yellich crossed the threshold. The interior of the pub smelled clean and fresh, heavy with polish and air freshener.

'Got to lock the door, sir,' the cleaner apologized, 'otherwise we'll get folk in wanting a drink before opening hours and then we'll be in trouble with the law.'

Hennessey said that they understood and he was interested that the cleaner should use the term 'we'. She clearly felt she belonged to 'The Arms', despite a very lowly position. She hurried away. Hennessey and Yellich stood in silence amongst the tables and chairs, which had been stacked to allow the carpet to be cleaned. Moments later a young man approached, bearded, dark hair, black shirt and trousers. 'Yes, gentlemen?'

'You are?'

'Graham, the under manager ... just racking the real ale. Andrew wants to get into the real ale market, but those guys ... regular drinkers, spill more than the real ale worshippers drink. Can't keep a business afloat if you can't sell the product ... got to move the product.'

'Is Mr Anglis in?'

'No ... no ... he's away today ... his wife and children are away.'

'Do you know where?'

'At his father-in-law's ... his son's tenth birthday has coincided with his parents-in-laws' wedding anniversary, more than the silver, less than the gold ... so they are having an all-day bash ... not a big event ... just immediate family, but going on all day from ten a.m.'

'That will be the Prendergahst house?'

'Well, yes.' Graham nodded. 'The Minister for Trade and Industry. That's what's called marrying the boss's daughter, alright. I don't know where the house is ... sorry.'

'It's alright.' Hennessey nodded. 'That residence we will find very easily.'

'Very, very easily,' added Yellich.

The house stood four square and solid. It seemed to Hennessey to say 'self-confidence'. It stood in the centre of its own grounds and seemed to be raised on an area of higher ground, like an island in a green sea. It was of red brick and would, thought Hennessey, glow impressively when the sun struck at the appropriate angle. Virginia creeper groped up the left-hand side of the house almost to the eaves. Two tall chimneys stood, sentry-like, at either end of the roof. Yellich drew the car to a halt in front of the house, where also were parked other motorcars, all prestigious makes, with Mercedes Benz, Volvo and Alfa Romeo being particularly well represented. 'Some family,' Hennessey remarked as he got out of the car.

'Marrying the boss's daughter, as the under manager said.' Yellich closed the driver's door, leaving the window wound down. Sounds of childish merriment could be heard coming from the rear of the house. 'This is going to put the cat among the pigeons.'

'Which,' Hennessey replied, 'is what we hope for.'

The two officers approached the door. It was wooden, polished and studded with bolts. Hennessey pulled the metal ring set in the wall beside the door. Bells were heard to jangle within the house.

'How old?' Yellich glanced at the house.

'This house? Probably older than it looks ... probably eighteenth century, late seventeenth...'

'Late seventeenth.' Yellich smiled and pointed to a stone plaque set amid the bricks above and to the right of the door – 'Anno 1693' – and pondered that the building was already nearly one hundred years old by the time the United States had been established. 'Trust me to find the easy way to date a building.'

Hennessey smiled and then adopted a more sombre expression as a bolt was to be heard being drawn.

'Can I help you?' The owner of the voice was an athletic-looking woman in her twenties who wore a maid's outfit, black blouse with white cuffs, black skirt which hung below the knees, black stockings, black, sensible shoes. Hennessey reflected that she was fortunate that her duties kept her within the cool interior of the house. She would bake in the sun wearing that clothing. He was impressed by her self-possession, her calm, her poise, for one so young.

'Police ... DCI Hennessey and DS Yellich. We're here to see Mr Anglis. We understand he is here?'

'Yes, sir. If you'd like to come in?' She

stepped aside.

With no small sense of gratitude, Hennessey and Yellich stepped into the hallway of the house and instantly appreciated the coolness therein. The hallway was a room in its own right with armchairs set round a coffee table, upon a rug, which rested on the varnished floorboards. Original oil paintings hung on the walls, a glass chandelier swayed gently, high above the coffee table, as the cool air within the house escaped through the open doorway. The maid shut the door and invited Hennessey and Yellich to take a seat. She walked away down a corridor to the right of the entrance hall.

Hennessey and Yellich sat down and waited. A silence developed between them, neither having anything to say but both focussing on the forthcoming interview. The silence was broken by the heavy footfall of a man approaching the entrance hall from the corridor down which the maid had departed.

'Angry man,' Yellich observed.

'Oh, hope so.' Hennessey smiled. 'Angry men trip themselves up.'

Andrew Anglis emerged from the corridor, his face flushed with rage. 'What the hell is this?'

'This –' Hennessey stood – 'this, is police work.'

'A murder investigation.' Yellich also stood.

'But my father-in-law's house! My child's birthday party ... the day of my in-law's wedding anniversary ... Couldn't it wait?'

'No,' Hennessey said. 'It can't wait. Is there somewhere we could talk? For your sake ... this is a little ... a little open ... but we are happy here if you are.'

'No ... no...' Anglis shook his head. 'Walls and woodlands have ears. We'll go in there.' He pointed to a door to the left of the entrance hall, opposite the corridor. 'It's where ... well, where anybody who comes to the house is seen.' He strode across the floor and opened the door, twisting the thigh-high handle aggressively. 'Please...' He held the door open and Hennessey and Yellich entered the room. A table surrounded by upright chairs stood by the tall windows; deeper in the room were armchairs and a settee; a large canvas showing a rural scene hung over a fireplace.

'So, what is it?' Anglis sat down at the table and with a flurry of his arm, invited the two officers to do the same.

'You are aware we are investigating a murder?'

'A suspicious death, you said, when you called on me a few days ago … and I told you all I know then.'

'Well, now it's a murder committed by members of the Dungeon Kings biker gang.' Yellich took out his notebook.

'Of which you were one.' Hennessey leaned forward, resting his arms on the tabletop. 'And it's now two murders.'

'Two?'

'Amanda Fryston,' Hennessey explained.

'Mandy? But Harry the Horse was convicted for that.'

'Yes … but we are taking a second look at it.' Hennessey explained. 'Somewhat to our shame, it might have been a wrongful conviction, so it needs a second look.'

Anglis began to pale, his anger seemed to evaporate.

'So,' Yellich added, 'we are looking at two murders … boyfriend and girlfriend … both in the same gang, both disappeared within three weeks of each other, but Harry Turner a.k.a. Harry the Horse didn't do both. He was locked up under suspicion of murdering Mandy when Terry North failed to come home one night. So, we can't pin both on Harry the Horse.'

'We've been finding out about the gang,' Hennessey spoke softly. 'Quite active.'

'Just a bit of fun, really...'

'Oh, it was more than that ... a lot more. We know about the heroin, the courier business ... picking it up from the docks, giving it to a guy who drove a Jaguar with number plate 771 WJ ... we know about the argument between Harry Turner and a gang member called Animal'

'Stefan...'

'Yes. He had enough pull with the Dungeon Master to get Harry Turner fitted up for the Mandy Fryston murder ... or so we are beginning to think. What say you?'

'Twenty years...' Anglis groaned.

'Your past is catching up with you, Mr Anglis.'

'Is it?' Anglis shot a hard glance at Hennessey.

'Isn't it?' Hennessey remained calm. 'Got

in a little too deep, you and your girlfriend, now your wife?'

'Did we?' Again that look of anger in Anglis's eyes.

'Possibly. You see this is what we think happened. There was a gang of biker boys and their chicks, a.k.a. girlfriends.' Hennessey spoke softly and held eye contact with Anglis, noting the man's jaw to be set firm, his eyes ablaze with anger; a man with a past, a man with something to hide. 'They had fun, broke a few motoring laws here and there, like doing seventy-four miles in ... whatever time it was which, over the route in question, could not have been achieved without excessive speed ... dangerously excessive. And perhaps a rumble with a rival gang now and again. Some serious assaults against any girl who wanted to leave the gang ... and one or two gang members got known for crimes committed independently of the gang but, in the main, all low-key except possibly in respect of the assaults on the girls who wanted out ... but they were not going to press charges. The bikers were so noisy, annoying the middle-aged and middle-class citizenry, but not the sort of criminal that the police then, or now, would be interested in unless they were caught red-handed perpetrating a felony. Right so far?'

Anglis shrugged his shoulders. He wasn't giving anything away.

'Inviting for a young man who wanted to rebel, and for his girlfriend who wanted to do the same. And you did the seventy-four miles ... and you were in.'

'So, is that something worth interrupting my son's birthday party for? Is that worth embarrassing me in front of my father-in-law? He has an election to fight soon ... he doesn't want the police at his house.'

'Well, the past, it is said, casts very long shadows ... very long ... and we are investigating a murder.'

'Two,' Yellich said with a smile. 'Two murders, sir.'

'Yes, I forgot ... two murders.'

'And a drug dealer who drove a Jaguar with a distinctive number plate, 771 WJ.'

'Yes ... I am getting old ... old for a police officer.' Hennessey smiled apologetically. 'You see how my younger colleague has to remind me? My pension's calling my name.

Not one murder but two, and a Class A drug dealer who was delivered of his drugs by members of the Dungeon Kings. Those were the waters you swam in all those years ago when you were looking for rebellious action. You might have left those waters ... but they haven't left you.'

'What do you mean?'

'Ten, twenty, thirty years ago ... matters not ... murder is murder ... conspiracy to supply heroin, is still conspiracy to supply heroin.'

Anglis glanced out of the window. Hennessey thought he looked unwell.

'The organization ticked over ... nicely ... and your boss, the gang leader, Richard Hawson, a.k.a. the Dungeon Master, was getting his foot in the door of organized crime in the Vale ... an efficient and reliable brick delivery system.'

'Brick?'

'Of heroin ... a brick of heroin ... about the size of a house brick in uncut form, easily transportable, but when cut with battery acid and bicarbonate of soda would have sufficient street value to make a serious bid for the purchase of this house.'

'I doubt it,' Anglis smirked. It was, Hennessey thought, the first crack. He had begun to talk.

'So you know about the heroin smuggling?'

'Possibly ... but knowing about it isn't a crime.'

'Well failing to report it is, but we are after bigger fish. So, let's press on. Now, as I said, it's all ticking over very smoothly for Hawson, then disaster ... a brick goes missing ... a brick that was being transported by Terry North and Amanda Fryston. The brick, incidentally, was found under Terry's bed in his room at his elderly parents' house ... still there, after all these years. Mr and Mrs North were keeping Terry's room "just so", in case he should return ... everything kept as he had left it. Good of them, don't you think?'

Anglis again glanced out of the window and shrugged. 'Possibly ... I never met them.'

Hardly the point, thought Hennessey, but he didn't comment. 'So, then things go awry for Hawson ... in fact they don't just go awry, they disintegrate, his credibility has gone. He owes the value of the brick to the guy in the Jaguar, and his heavies, not, fortunately for Hawson, the street value, but the uncut value ... though that is still a lot of dosh. Has to empty his little piggybank to buy off said guy with Jaguar ... avoid having his throat cut and his body thrown into the Ouse. That must have hurt ... but what hurts more was that he was a nobody again, and indeed he never got back into organized crime ... a few petty offences. Now he is presently inside for assault.'

'Well, all very interesting, but what has it got to do with me?'

'We are coming on to that. You might not believe it, Andrew ... you don't mind if I call you Andrew?'

Anglis shook his head.

'You might not believe it, but we might be doing you a favour.'

'Oh?' Anglis looked alert, interested – very interested.

'It was silly, stupid ... stupid beyond com-prehension that Terry North and Amanda Fryston could think they could steal that brick of heroin and tell the Dungeon Master and his lieutenants, Animal, Ranker and

Soldier, that they had *lost* it and assume that would be the end of the matter.'

'Well, they were both pretty well brain-dead.'

'So you know what happened?'

'Well, yes ... since you know anyway ... yes.'

'So what did happen?'

'I only heard rumours. What is the favour you mentioned?'

'Well, it's really the favour you can do yourself, Andrew.'

'Meaning?'

'Well, you have a lot to lose ... the pub, the University Arms, that is going to make you a wealthy man. There's big money in the licensed retail trade, so I hear.'

'There can be ... if you get a paying pub. Yes, you can retire very comfortably off ... and retire early, too.'

'And this.' Hennessey looked around him. 'Your father-in-law, cabinet member ... an election in the offing.'

'Oh...' Anglis put his hand to his head. 'This could not come at a worse time. Publicity like this could ruin him ... could even cost us the election.'

'So anything you can do to help us ... that will help you.'

'*That's* the favour?'

'Yes. Now we think – we know – Hawson orchestrated the murders of Terry North and Amanda Fryston ... even if he didn't do them himself. Anything you can help us with, Andrew ... and your name doesn't have to be mentioned...'

'Oh...' Anglis looked from left to right. 'Oh, what a mess.'

'Largely a mess of your own making.'

'I can't tell you what happened to Terry North or Amanda ... I mean who did it, but the guy in the Jag, his name was, probably still is, Pickworth.'

'Pickworth.' Yellich wrote on his notepad. 'First name?'

'Donald ... Donald Pickworth. He'll be in his mid-fifties now.'

'Did you deliver a brick or two?'

'Not that I'll admit to, not in a proper interview on tape in the cop shop ... certainly not sign a statement to that effect, but yes ... a couple. It was part of the thrill, you see ... not for the money but for the thrill of doing something illegal. You think like that when you're twenty years old.'

'I didn't,' Hennessey said.

'Neither did I,' Yellich added. 'Neither did I.'

'Do you know if Donald Pickworth is still in York?'

'Yes, I used to see him from time to time. Seemed to be doing alright ... flash cars, flash looking women in the passenger seat. Haven't seen him for quite a while, though. Don't know where he lives now.'

Hennessey stood, then resumed his seat. 'Oh ... yes ... I know what I was going to ask. Animal, Ranker, Soldier ... how did you get along with them?'

'OK ... they were gang members ... OK ... we got on well.'

'You see that's not what we heard.'

'Oh?'

'Yes. You and a bloke called the Mad Accountant seemed to enjoy protection from the Dungeon Master because you were a bit posh, gave the Dungeon Kings a bit of class ... so he thought, but his second in command didn't like you ... or the Mad Accountant.'

'Had it in for you,' Yellich added. 'Both

of you.'

'Wanted to do something to make you prove yourself, prove that you were hard men ... and when the brick was stolen, and the Master lost his street cred, there would have been a power struggle ... an authority challenge. The Master no longer had the power. What happened then? Did the power pass to Animal and the other two?'

'No, as you've just said, the Master ordered ... he still had the power.'

'But not as much ... he had to give in a little to Animal and Ranker and Soldier. So, what happened?'

'I'd like you to leave now. Just go ... please...' Anglis hung his head.

'Alright.' Hennessey stood. Yellich did likewise, 'But don't go too far away, this case is cracking wide open.'

'Wide open,' Yellich added. 'We'll likely be back.'

'Unless, of course, you come to us first.'

In the car, driving slowly away, Hennessey said, 'Comments?'

'Didn't tell us anything we wouldn't have found out anyway.'

'Nope.'

'Frightened him though.'

'Yes.' Hennessey glanced out of the window at the neat flowerbeds and manicured lawn of the grounds of the home of the Right Hon. Robert Prendergahst MP. 'Yes, we did that alright. With a bit of luck he'll now start running round in circles.'

'So what now, boss? The Mad Accountant?'

'Oh, I think so ... call on him at his office again. Methought he was a bit too anxious for us to call on him at home. Ventnor and Webster believed they'd shaken him ... time for us to shake a little more. Do you remember his workplace address?'

'Adams and Co.'

'Yes ... that was it ... on Skeldergate.' Hennessey glanced at his watch. 'You know, he might just care to join us for lunch.'

Yellich smiled. 'Oh that would be so exquisitely civilized. What a civilized way to interview a suspect.'

The man's first reaction was anger. The Environmental Health people are quite clear, he thought, their flyers are very clear. Before burning garden rubbish, ensure none of your neighbours are using their gardens for drying washing or recreation. Do not burn toxic matter, avoid hot and humid conditions when the air is still and the smoke can't easily escape. Here he was, hanging out washing, clear as clear can be and that ... that ... newcomer, he has a garden fire on a day like this. He turned in his anger and saw that he was right, the smoke was coming from the new neighbour's property and it was black toxic smoke ... but it wasn't a small fire in the garden, by the time he saw the fire it had caught hold, with black smoke billowing out of the windows.

'It's bad enough you come to the office again,' Bannister exclaimed with a voice that shook with emotion. 'I told your two colleagues I would be happy to see you at my home. What was wrong with that?' He flung the menu down. 'I insist on buying my own.'

'Happy or happier?' Hennessey glanced over the menu. 'Pasta, pasta or pasta? Hobson's choice.'

'Well, you thought Italian, sir. You could have a steak ... but it's a bit pricey.'

'And too heavy for lunchtime ... no ... I'll have the beef lasagne.'

' "Happy or happier?" ' Bannister glared at Hennessey, who sat opposite him. 'What's that supposed to mean?'

'Well, happier to talk to the police in the privacy of your own home on safer, more solid ground away from the prying eyes of your colleagues ... especially your employers.'

'Twice in a week ... now they are going to demand to know what is going on.'

'What will you tell them?'

Bannister shook his head. 'Why are you doing this to me? This is harassment.'

'Having lunch with you is harassment? Oh, come now ... I hardly think so.' Hennessey spoke in a warm, gentle manner.

'You are pressurizing me.'

'Which is our job.' Hennessey glanced about him. It was a neat restaurant, he thought, very old York with its narrow frontage but extending back a long way from the street, polished pine furniture, string upholstered chairs, framed photographs of Rome, Venice, Sienna and Florence decorating the varnished brick walls, small potted plants on each table, a wine rack behind the counter. There had been very few patrons in the restaurant when he, Yellich and a bemused, and worried looking, John Bannister, asked for an out-of-the-way table in an alcove. 'It's what we get paid to do … pressurize people.'

'We're quite good at it, too,' Yellich added, with a smile.

'I don't see how I can help you. I told the other two officers all I know.'

'You see, John…' Hennessey leaned back in his chair. 'You don't mind if I call you John?'

Bannister shook his head.

'Good … we do like to keep things as friendly as possible.'

'No need to be uncivilized about this.' Again Yellich smiled.

'None at all,' Hennessey added, 'none at all … but you see we don't think it's true that you have told us – "us" being the police – told us all you do know.'

Bannister glanced at Hennessey but said nothing.

'You see, we have just visited your old biker friend, Andrew Anglis. You are a bit put out that we called on you at your place of work at lunchtime ... I rather think Mr Anglis was more put out that we called on him at his father-in-law's house.'

'His father-in-law's?' Bannister gasped.

'Yes ... oh, yes ... interrupted a children's birthday party and might have put a bit of a dampner on a wedding anniversary dinner as well.'

'But that's the long arm of the law–' Yellich tore at a piece of garlic bread – 'it can reach up and down the social scale and across oceans and all over the European Union, courtesy of the European arrest warrant.'

'So, to the home of the Right Hon. Robert Prendergahst MP is but a stone's throw ... and your place of work even closer.' Hennessey too helped himself to a piece of bread.

'So what do you mean, I haven't told you everything?'

'Well ... even though we are talking about events of some twenty years ago, this has proved to be a rapidly evolving investigation. We know pretty well all the things you might be happy for us to know about the biker gang ... the seventy-four and other pretty harmless stuff ... but supposing we tell you that we know about the courier operation the Dungeon Master set up, running bricks of heroin from London and Hull docks into York?'

Bannister swallowed and began to pale.

'Suppose we told you about the connection with a local heavy called Donald Pickworth ... the receiver of the bricks, whom we have still to interview but we know he's still in York ... and supposing we tell you we know about the lost brick around which time Terry North and Amanda Fryston were murdered.' Hennessey paused to sip a glass of water.

'We also know –' Yellich picked up the thread – 'that you were protected by the Dungeon Master ... you and Anglis both. He thought you added a touch of class to the gang ... for some reason he was impressed by your background, but his three right-hand men, Animal, Soldier and Ranker, were not so impressed and when that brick was lost, you were not so protected. The Dungeon Master was out of the big league and that meant the Kings were just boys on toys again.'

'Then there was a power bid, a leadership challenge,' Hennessey continued, 'which Richard Hawson, the Dungeon Master, survived but the suggestion is he had to give something to his second-in-command, who wanted you and Anglis to prove yourselves, or get a good kicking. So, we want to know about the murder of Terry North and Amanda Fryston. They were murdered on Hawson's orders for stealing the brick of heroin, but he wouldn't get his hands dirty ... so we're offering to help those who help us.'

'I have a future,' Bannister spoke meekly. 'I am going to be made a partner. I have a fiancée...'

'You also have a past,' Hennessey said. 'You also have a history. We haven't chatted to Animal yet, or Ranker or Soldier ... but we will soon ... this afternoon, tomorrow ... that sort of soon, think hours ... not days ... not weeks, but hours. We can't promise anything but the first one that talks and makes a statement, and agrees to give evidence, will be doing himself a huge favour.'

'A massive favour,' Yellich added. 'I mean

"self-help" just isn't the expression.'

An Italian waiter in a red shirt and black trousers approached the table and in a warm, friendly manner asked them if they were ready to order.

'The lasagne for me, please,' Hennessey said, handing the waiter the menu.

'The risotto.' Yellich also handed the waiter his menu. 'Thank you.'

Bannister slid sideways from his chair and left the restaurant.

'He's not feeling well,' Hennessey explained. 'It's a bit of a bad day for him.'

'Ah...' The waiter raised his arms. 'We all have them.'

'Indeed,' Hennessey said with a smile. 'Indeed we do.'

'Anything to drink, gentlemen?'

Hennessey glanced at Yellich. 'I know we shouldn't, but I scent victory.'

'So do I, sir.' Yellich smiled.

'Good.' He turned to the waiter. 'Just a half carafe of house red, thank you.'

'Just paying a call,' Ventnor said with a smile.

'Trying to meet all the old gang,' added

Webster.

Zielinski curled a lip in contempt. He stood square in the doorway of his house, long-haired, unkempt beard, hairy chest, stomach overhanging the belt of his jeans. His arms were heavily tattooed. A small boy, about ten years old, thought Ventnor, came up and stood beside him. 'Get in the room,' Zielinski snarled and the small boy ran into the interior of the house.

'So, we're paying a call.'

'About what?' Zielinski leaned against the doorway of his house.

'Oh, about this and that,' Webster said and smiled. 'You remember the old gang...? Do they still call you Animal? The Dungeon Master, Richard Hawson ... then there was Soldier and Ranker ... or should I say Norbert Strubby and Philip Heath.'

'The Coffin Dodger is no more,' Ventnor added, 'but you will know that.'

'I heard.' Zielinski eyed the officers with undisguised distaste and suspicion. 'None of us dodge it forever.'

'Then there was Camel ... what was his name? Shane Smithson ... was that it?'

'Aye...'

'And Harry the Horse.'

At the mention of Turner's name, Zielinski's eyes narrowed, just briefly for a split second, but they definitely narrowed and both officers noticed it.

'Then there were the two posh ones –' Ventnor glanced at Webster – 'what were they called?'

'Anglis and Bannister.'

'That's it ... both doing alright ... you'll know that. Anglis has the University Arms and Bannister's a chartered accountant.'

'What's this about? I haven't seen them kids in twenty years.'

'Do you still ride?'

'Yes ... that's my bike.' Zielinski nodded to a motorcycle which stood beside his house and which was covered in a plastic sheet. 'It never leaves you.'

'You haven't taken a ride out to see Harry the Horse?'

Zielinski shook his head. 'No ... don't know where he lives. Haven't taken a ride anywhere ... not for a while.' He stepped forwards and walked to his motorcycle and lifted the tarpaulin, 'No cylinder head,' he said.

The officers looked at the machine. The top half of the engine was indeed missing.

'Live on benefits,' Zielinski explained as he let the tarpaulin fall. 'I can't afford a new head, got to wait for a used one. I have a wire in with a guy who breaks bikes. He gets heads in for Honda 500s but a lot need so much decoking. He'll tell me when he gets a decent one in ... until then ... no riding for me. So, what's this about?'

'It's about the gang,' Ventnor said and smiled. 'About the good old days.'

'You've got a lot of priors.' Webster glanced about him; a council estate, a small overgrown garden, small houses in regimented streets, children who eyed the officers with the same sort of hostility and suspicion that Zielinski eyed them, each already well on their way to their criminal records and none over the age of ten, so far as Webster could tell in his brief glance. A bead of sweat trickled down his neck from his scalp. The air on the estate was pungent, as if a sewer had overflowed or a gas main had fractured, but none of the residents seemed to notice anything amiss. 'But all small scale stuff,' Webster continued. 'You were more of a social nuisance than a criminal, which is why we are calling on you ... see this as a favour.'

'You're doing my head in, you're talking in riddles. What is this?'

'What's the longest you've been inside? Sentenced to nine months for receiving ... out in four.'

'We do our homework, you see,' Ventnor added. 'I mean, you're a big guy, you're in your forties, you'll survive twenty years in top security more easily than a younger fella would.'

'But then you'll be in your sixties when you breathe free air again and your little lad there ... he'll be married with his own family,' Webster pressed.

Colour drained from Zielinski's face. 'What are you talking about? Twenty years? I'm clean ... I've turned the corner. I haven't been to court for anything for ten years ... more.'

'Oh, we know ... we know...'

'So, what's the grief for? I'm a solid citizen now.'

'Yes, that's why we are calling on you first. You see, we know about the bricks of heroin the Dungeon Kings carried from the docks for Richard Hawson and how he delivered them to a guy called Pickworth ... and we know about the murder of Terry North ... and we don't think that Harry Turner a.k.a. Harry the Horse murdered Amanda Fryston, so we are looking at that murder again.'

'Closely,' added Ventnor, 'very closely.'

'We also know about the biker code of not grassing on your mates ... but our top boss and our sergeant are calling on Anglis and Bannister while we call on you and Soldier and Ranker because you were the top dogs in the gang. Causey Jones and the Mad Builder, they're small fry ... and the lasses like Felicity Gaol Bait Appleyard and posh Angela Prendergahst ... well, they know nothing, but you and Ranker and Soldier ... We're closing in, and code or no code, the first one to give information ... I mean, something we don't know...'

'Or wouldn't find out ourselves, anyway,' Ventnor growled.

'Yes,' Webster added. 'Or wouldn't find out ourselves ... well, that person is doing himself a huge, huge favour.'

'Huge favour,' echoed Webster. 'Huge.'

'Think it over.' Ventnor handed him a calling card. 'That's me ... that's the phone number ... or walk in off the street ... Micklegate Bar. Take care.'

The officers turned and walked back down the pitted concrete path of Stefan Zielinski's council house.

The senior fire officer at the incident stood beside his deputy, both viewed the shrunken, twisted corpse with grim expressions. They had both seen it before, but it never got any easier. 'Could be suicide...'

'Probably ... not for us to say. I'll let the police know.'

The man knew he had to prepare himself. He had heard that ghosts and poltergeists were the spirits of those who had met an unexpected death, who had had no time to prepare themselves. It is why he had further learned there are never any ghosts in hospices, because the patients therein spend their days preparing for their end. He knew that if he was going to do it, he must achieve a state of mind where he can find beauty in a blade of grass. He must go willingly towards the light.

It was Thursday, the twentieth of June, 13.10 hours.

Seven

Thursday, 20 June, 14.35 hours – 17.47 hours
*in which a dreadful death is discovered, two
men ponder their imminent fall from grace and
the kind reader hears of one already fallen.*

Yellich slowed the car to a halt behind the black, windowless mortuary van. Beyond the van was a marked police vehicle, beyond that three fire appliances which completely blocked the narrow rural road. Opposite the mortuary van was an unmarked car, beside which stood Webster and Ventnor, both wearing solemn expressions. 'I did think we'd be returning here, boss–' Yellich halted the vehicle and applied the handbrake – 'just not in these circumstances.'

'Aye.' Hennessey said nothing else. Somerled Yellich had spoken for both of them. He left the car. As he did so, Webster and

236

Ventnor approached.

'Afternoon, sir.' Ventnor spoke with a solemn tone. 'Suspicious death ... one male ... the uniforms attended with the fire crew ... the Fire Service found one corpse within, notified the constable who phoned Micklegate Bar. Myself and Reg ... I mean DC Webster, were the only CID in the building, so we attended ... left a message for you, sir.'

'Yes ... as you see, we got it.'

'SOCO is in the building. Dr Mann has pronounced life extinct so we called the pathologist. There is no further risk of combustion.'

'Gathered.' Hennessey smiled. 'Otherwise the police surgeon and SOCO wouldn't have been allowed in there.' He looked at the burned out cottage, blackened, marbled timbers, roof collapsed into the wall shell.

'Excuse me, sir,' Webster spoke hesitatingly, 'but isn't this address...?'

'Yes, it is.' Hennessey anticipated him. 'This is the home ... this *was* the home of Harry the Horse Turner.' He paused. 'We had hoped to bring him good news. What is known, apart from the fact it was arson? I can still smell petrol...'

'Well, yes, sir ... arson. The gentleman in the next cottage down raised the alarm, but only when the house was well alight. He didn't see anybody or anything suspicious.'

'Have you seen the body?'

'Yes, sir ... it's chained to a chair, empty petrol can beside it. The fire officer wondered if it was suicide.'

Hennessey shook his head. 'No, it's not suicide, Harry had a lot to live for; he was on the verge of being exonerated for the murder of Amanda Fryston ... we should have taken him into protective custody.'

'We offered to, skipper ... he refused.'

'We should have arrested him for something, for his own good.' Hennessey shook his head. 'That lunch doesn't taste so pleasant now ... to think we were celebrating while this was happening ... middle of the day as well.' He turned to Ventnor and Webster. 'What did you do this forenoon?'

Webster related the details of the visit to Stefan Animal Zielinski and his crumbling council house on a malodorous estate.

'I see.'

'We had planned to visit Soldier and Ranker this afternoon, sir,' Webster explain-

238

ed, 'as agreed, to apply pressure ... let it be known that the first one to give information...'

'Yes, DS Yellich and I did the same thing to Anglis and Bannister, also this morning. We thought we might have got a result with Bannister and allowed ourselves a pleasant luncheon ... confess the words "chicken" and "hatch" come to mind.'

'Still might, sir,' Yellich offered.

'Probably ... but we could have done without this.' He waved a finger at the smouldering remains of the bungalow. 'This is not just the murder of Harry Turner because he was spilling the beans, this was a warning to anybody else who might want to help themselves by giving information.' Hennessey glanced to his right, beyond the fire appliances at a television crew with lighting and sound equipment, at photographers and reporters scribbling on notepads. 'This will be on the TV news this evening ... and in the papers tomorrow.' He glanced around him at the flat fields, lush with corn, the occasional bungalow, the equally occasional stand of trees. 'What's that proverb, Yellich? Fourteenth-century English? You have quoted it before ... about fields and woods?'

'"The fields have eyes, the woods have ears"?'

'Yes, that's the one. Look at the field of view round here ... flat, flat as a billiard table ... houses in full view ... a man on a tractor over there, see, in the distance? I do not believe—'

'Pathologist, sir,' Yellich interrupted Hennessey. 'Sorry, sir, but Dr D'Acre has arrived.'

Hennessey turned and saw a 1947 red and white Riley RMA approach the scene, the chrome glinting in the sun.

'Lovely car,' muttered Ventnor, wiping the sweat from his brow.

Yellich smiled. 'She told me once she always has it serviced by the same garage and the proprietor has made her promise him first refusal should she ever sell it. She was happy to give it because she intends to bequeath it to her son in the fullness of time, having inherited it from her father.'

'Really?' Ventnor returned the smile.

'Yes, really. So the proprietor gives excellent service, hoping that the machine will one day belong to him.'

'Bit unfair, letting him live in hope of something that will never be realized.'

'Oh, she has told the proprietor of her intentions but he has still insisted on first refusal.'

'Alright!' Hennessey turned round. 'As I was saying, I refuse to believe that no one saw anything, not on a clear day like this, excellent visibility, houses and land workers dotted about. So ... Webster and Ventnor...?'

'Sir?'

'House-to-house ... or rather remote cottage-to-remote cottage, and agricultural workers in the fields, people walking their dogs or riding their bikes ... question everybody.'

'Yes, sir?'

'Visit Ranker and Soldier later.'

'Very good, sir.'

'Yellich.'

'Sir?'

'Take a trip out to Full Sutton, find out who's been visiting Richard the Dungeon Master Hawson or who he has been communicating with.'

'Yes, sir.'

'I'll remain here, get a lift back to York

with someone, somehow.'

Hennessey waited until Dr D'Acre approached him and touched the brim of his panama. 'Afternoon, ma'am. Can I carry your bag for you?'

Louise D'Acre handed her Gladstone bag to Hennessey. 'Thank you, Chief Inspector.'

'This way, ma'am.' Hennessey led the way up the path to the charred shell that was Harry Turner's cottage. He glanced around the cottage as he stepped his feet over the threshold and saw that it had clearly been a fierce conflagration. It was, he found, unrecognizable as the cottage that he and Yellich had stood in just a day or two earlier. All that could burn, had burned, the location was just a mess of blackened, charred and marbled timber in the centre of which was the remains of Harry Turner. He had, it seemed, shrunk, so much so that flesh had burned to the bone, his mouth was pulled in a dreadful grin, his wrists were fastened to what had clearly been a wooden chair, with padlocks and chains. The Scene of Crime officers stepped back reverentially as Hennessey and Dr D'Acre approached.

'Death was pronounced by the police

surgeon a short time ago.' Hennessey spoke softly as he looked at the corpse. 'A formality in this case ... I think you'll agree?'

'Oh, yes,' Dr D'Acre said with a nod of her head, 'but an important one. Do you know him?'

'Well, he is unrecognizable but we believe it to be the corpse of one Harry Turner ... he was known to us, possibly a wrongfully convicted person on the point of establishing his innocence.'

'Oh ... that is a tragedy.'

'Yes, but that is why we'll be treating this as murder. The fire officers pondered suicide. It isn't really uncommon for someone to chain themselves up so they can't escape, then douse themselves in petrol and flick a lighter or strike a match, but Harry – if it is Harry, and it will be – but Harry had everything to live for. He was certain he was going to be vindicated.'

'Well, establish identity, that will be the first task. He's known to you, you say. Had he been in prison?'

'Yes, for murder. He told us he admitted his guilt in prison in order to work towards a parole. He wanted out before the system destroyed him. It was his plan then to set about establishing his innocence.'

'I see. So he was in prison for a few years?'

'Yes, ma'am.'

'So, his dental records will be on file? That's what we'll use to establish his identity, then we'll turn our attention to the cause of death.'

'I have a feeling that it will be that he was incinerated alive. He was about to give information ... turn Queen's evidence ... he was going to be instrumental in sending some very heavy boys to prison for a long time ... for a murder ... possibly two murders that they thought they had got away with, and had got away with for twenty years.'

'Ah ... I can see why someone would want to silence him ... but why be so brutal? What did that prove?'

'Well, it would have sent a message to any others who might want to help themselves, which we are presently doing our best to persuade one or two people to do.'

'Well ... I can do little here. Don't pin me down on time of death, you and I have danced that dance before.'

'Indeed.'

'As I have said, he died some time after he was last seen alive by a reliable witness and sometime before his body was found, and that is as close as medical knowledge can get.'

'Understood.'

'There is little point in taking a rectal temperature, too much thermal confusion and there is no ground temperature to take ... so ... if you have finished, taken all the photographs you need, then you can arrange for the deceased to be conveyed to York District Hospital. I'll perform the post-mortem as soon as he arrives. I have a clear schedule at the moment.' She allowed herself a rare smile and very brief eye contact with Hennessey. 'Not many suspicious or unexplained deaths in York and its environs lately.'

'Calm before the storm,' Hennessey replied, for want of something to say.

'Hope you're wrong there.'

'Actually, so do I.' He raised an eyebrow. 'So do I.'

'So ... will you be observing for the police?'

'Yes, my officers are on other duties, all related to this.' He looked at the black, grinning corpse. 'This has overall priority.'

'Had quite a few visits in the last few days.' The assistant governor was a young man, smartly dressed, bespectacled and had what Yellich thought to be a serious attitude. He found it difficult to imagine this man smiling or displaying any lightness of heart. He had not enjoyed the drive out to Full Sutton; he felt for Harry Turner, his death, especially as awful as it seemed to be, and he found himself hoping that the man had at least been rendered unconscious before the accelerant was fired.

Yellich had parked his car in the visitors' car park and walked towards the reception office, noting the light blue flag of Her Majesty's Prison Service hanging limply on the flagpole against the darker blue of the sky. He had explained the reason for his visit and was escorted to the office of Assistant Governor Bainbridge. Bainbridge invited him to take a seat and picked up the phone on his desk requesting the file on Richard Hawson to be brought to him. When it was brought by a uniformed officer, Bainbridge opened it at the most recent recording and said that Hawson had had quite a few visits in the last few days. 'He has been using all his permitted visiting orders but none have gone to family members, which is a break from the usual pattern. He was last visited by one Stefan Zielinski.'

'Yes, we know him ... he is a very relevant character in our investigation.'

'I see. He was also visited by a Norbert Strubby...'

'Also known as Soldier.' Yellich smiled. 'And I'll wager one Philip Heath was also a recent visitor?'

'Yes...' Assistant Governor Bainbridge remained solemn of character. 'Yes, you'd wager safely. He is also of interest to you?'

'Yes ... also known as Ranker. When did they visit?'

'Yesterday, the day before, and the day before that.'

'I see. Yes, that is an interesting pattern.'

'Well, inmates are only allowed a certain number of visiting orders per month and they usually spread them out ... one visit a week, for example and they usually go to family ... or close friends. We have no record of those three gentlemen visiting for a very long time ... and then they visit on consecutive days, it means something is afoot ... some plan is being hatched. We monitor letters, of course, both incoming and outgoing ... nothing of concern was noted otherwise we'd have been in contact with the police.'

'Yes...'

'But there are two channels of communication which we can't monitor ... visits and other inmates' visits. Messages can get passed from visitor to inmate and vice versa ... but also an inmate can ask another inmate to give a message to his visitor to give to a third person on the outside.'

'I see.'

'And that traffic is widespread. Getting things in and out of prison is skilful and inventive. Heroin and cocaine wraps, usually by kissing ... but also mobile phones ... tobacco ... if they can get that stuff in. Getting information in and out by word of mouth is child's play. So these three visits, they will be the tip of an iceberg of communication about a certain issue...'

'I see ... interesting ... and the other interesting thing is that he has not requested any further visiting orders ... so, job done, whatever the job was.'

'We think we know what that was.'

'Oh?'

'Yes ... the murder of one Harold Turner. He had indicated that he was prepared to give evidence against Richard Hawson.'

'That is interesting.'

'I'd like to see him.'

'Hawson?'

'Yes.'

'Alone? The police usually visit in pairs.'

'It won't be an interview ... it will be me giving him information ... time for him to sweat.'

'Certainly.' Assistant Governor Bainbridge reached for his telephone.

The man and woman walked side by side, arm in arm, along the banks of the Ouse at St George's Field. All around them individuals and families were at their recreation, enjoying the day, with children running on the grass, couples strolling, individuals standing by the railings observing the pleasure craft on the river.

'Something's bothering you,' the woman

said softly. 'I can tell.'

The man remained silent.

'There can be no secrets, if we are keeping secrets from each other already...'

'No ... it's just ... something at work.' John Bannister glanced at his watch. 'I'm late, I must get back ... this is only supposed to be a lunch break.'

The charred body of Harold Turner lay on its side on the stainless steel dissecting table, as Dr D'Acre, assisted by Eric Filey, used a steel rod to prise open the jaw of the deceased. The jaw gave with a loud crack and Dr D'Acre and Eric Filey stood back and wiped layers of burned flesh from their hands. It came away, Hennessey thought, like a well cooked joint, the meat just melting from the bone.

'It's early twenty-first century–' Louise D'Acre placed the metal bar on the instrument tray – 'and they still haven't improved on the lever. "Give me a place to stand and I will move the world" ... or whatever it was. The lever and the wheel ... can't do without them. Well, let us see what we shall see.' She peered into the mouth of the deceased, holding a thin pencil torch and then stepped back. 'Oh...' She steadied herself. 'Oh ... this is bad.'

At the edge of the laboratory, Hennessey, dressed head to foot in green paper disposable coveralls, involuntarily took a step forward but remained silent as protocol dictated; it was for him to speak when spoken to.

'This is a bit bad.' Dr D'Acre raised her voice and turned to Hennessey. 'Not only was he alive when he was burned ... but there is thermal damage to the inside of the mouth. He was conscious ... his mouth was open and the flames were licking at him in there.'

'Oh...' Hennessey groaned. 'As if he had been screaming?'

'Yes.' Dr D'Acre stepped closer to the body and felt along the legs and arms. 'The fact that he was conscious rules out any serious head injury that would have rendered him unconscious. The skull has split, which appears to be the result of injury, but in fact is clearly caused by heat expansion of the tissue. There is also a heat haematoma, which has allowed the brain to seep out of the skull ... but all peri- or post-mortem. His arms are not raised as much as I would have expected them to be and so this indicates that he was restrained. I did notice padlocks and chains on the deceased at the scene of the crime.'

'Yes...'

'Someone really did not like this person.' Dr D'Acre rested her hands on the side of the dissection table. 'There is real vindictiveness ... real malice here.'

Hennessey remained silent. He noticed that Eric Filey, normally able to raise the levity of the pathology laboratory with tasteful and appropriate humour, was particularly subdued. This death had reached him.

'He was restrained,' Dr D'Acre said, 'doused with accelerant, probably petrol, and set on fire ... while conscious.' She turned to Hennessey. 'I do hope you apprehend the person or persons responsible for this, Chief Inspector.'

'I hope we do too, ma'am.' Hennessey spoke grimly. 'I hope we do too.'

'I'll remove the jaw, send the lower dentures to Wetherby, they can match them with the dental records of Mr...?'

'Turner.' Hennessey pronounced the name with respect. 'Harold Turner. I will supply Wetherby with his details so an ID can be confirmed. But it will be he.'

Yellich thought Richard Hawson looked smug. He sat back in his chair in the interview room with his arms folded and eyed Yellich with a knowing smile and a gleam in his eye. 'I thought you visited in pairs,' he said.

'That's what Mr Bainbridge asked.' Yellich too relaxed in his chair. 'I told him it wasn't a formal interview.'

'Oh?' Hawson yawned and stretched his arms. 'What is it? A social call?'

'In fact you could say that. Since I was here checking on your visitors ... the ones over the last few days ... and since I was here, I thought I'd call to see you.'

'Oh, that's nice,' Hawson sneered, 'that's really, really nice.'

Yellich glanced up at the thick opaque brick of glass, which allowed natural light into the room. 'Well, I do want you to enjoy your stay here...'

'I won't be here too much longer, this is

just a brief visit.'

'You think?'

'I know. A few more weeks, then I'm breathing free air, drinking beer ... out on my bike ... especially that. Being banged up ... blokes in here miss different things ... women, booze ... their families in some cases, but me –' he briefly imitated driving a motorbike – 'there's no freedom like it ... tearing along at a hundred miles an hour. You know why I like it? I've analyzed it.'

'You have?'

'Yeah, I have ... learned that word in here ... analyze ... it's a good word. The chaplain asked us to analyze our actions, our deeds, or misdeeds ... had to go away and look it up, but it's a good word. Anyway, know why I ride? Why folks ride?'

'Tell me.'

'Because it requires total concentration. If you are totally concentrating it drives everything else from your mind, everything. People play bingo for the same reason...' Hawson put his hands behind his head.

'You reckon?'

'Yeah ... I worked that out myself. We play bingo in here and, when the screw says, "eyes down", it's total concentration ... it's very relaxing ... exactly the same as being on the bike. But when you're in your cell you can't sleep ... things just flood into your mind, you can't escape them no matter how much you toss and turn ... and you think of the world going on outside ... and you think how you've got one life and you're wasting it in here...'

'I'm so sorry for you.'

'Yeah, well, like I said ... I'm out of here soon.'

'Well, this is the reason why I felt I had to call on you, Mr Hawson ... give you a little update.'

'Oh...?'

'Nice job you did of Harry the Horse.'

'Hey –' Richard Hawson held his hands up – 'woah, I was in here ... what better alibi?'

'But it's interesting that you know what I'm talking about because the body was only found this morning ... not on the TV news or in the newspapers yet.'

Hawson flushed with anger.

'That's what's called an own goal, Richard.'

'There's just you and me … no witnesses.'

'That's true, but I can report it. I can let my boss know that you knew of Harry's murder before it was made public … it means we are on the right track.'

'Right track?'

'Yeah, you being visited by Ranker and Soldier … the gang is still together.'

'We keep in touch … bit old now, but yes, we keep in touch.'

'Is that because you know where all the bodies are buried?'

'Meaning?'

'You can't burn everybody, Richard…' Yellich paused and then said, 'Harry was torched because he was going to give evidence against you. He was happy to do that because you framed him for the murder of Amanda Fryston.'

'He 'fessed up to that.'

'Yes, only after he was convicted, only to get an early parole before the system ruined him. He knew that no one can survive for more than ten years maximum security … as you have said yourself, "Things just flood into your mind", I think you said and, what was it? "You think of the world going on outside"?' Yellich felt pleased to notice that Hawson suddenly looked markedly less smug than he had when he'd been brought to the interview room amid a rattle of chains and keys. 'So, what's the sketch? You hope to cover your tracks?'

Hawson shrugged.

'It only takes one to turn Queen's evidence, then you all go down.'

Hawson smirked. 'Off the record?'

'Off the record.'

'Nobody's going to crack. That's the point, you see, nobody will crack. Nobody wants to go down for life at our age ... not in their forties. In your twenties, you can come out after doing your ten and still have plenty to live for ... to work towards, but a nominal life sentence when you're forty-five ... even if you do ten...'

'It'll be more than ten. We're talking about two murders and a heroin supply racket ... twenty years before parole.'

Hawson's jaw dropped.

'Oh yes, we know about the courier business you set up, and how Mandy Stupid Girl Fryston, stole a brick from you and finished you in the crime game before you started.'

Hawson paled, then recovered his self-confidence. 'You see, you've just proved my point. That's twenty huge reasons why nobody will talk.'

'No ... it's twenty for those that don't talk, possibly as little as five for the first one that does talk.' Yellich paused. 'Do you want to help yourself? I can take a statement from you...'

Hawson stood and knocked on the door of the interview room. 'I'm saying nothing.'

'Well, should you change your mind when you can't sleep tonight, you know where we are.' Yellich also stood. 'You're clearly finding a few months difficult. How will you manage twenty years? Give it some thought.'

'There were bikers in the night.' The woman stood squarely in the doorway of her cottage. 'Made a right racket.'

'When was this, Mrs...?'

'Miss Oxterby. Never wed. Grew up in this cottage and I'll die in it. Took over the tenancy from my father. I work at Owen's Farm, same as he did ... tied cottage, you see. I work in the house ... domestic duties, you understand.'

'I see.'

'All my days...'

She was a stocky woman, healthy, fresh-faced complexion. Country living, thought Ventnor, definitely had its appeal.

'So, what did you see?' Ventnor probed.

'Not a lot ... it was dark ... night time. You can see the cottage from here, across two fields. Heard more than saw. City people don't realize the distance sound can travel if all else is quiet enough. The number of conversations I've listened to when people thought I was too far away to overhear. There were men and women ... three men ... at least one female ... on three motorbikes. Damn noisy machines. There was some shouting, a fight, then it went quiet again.'

'What time was this ... about?'

'Exactly midnight, the bells from the church in Tusham were chiming. Five miles away but you can hear them on a still night, especially in winter when the ground is hard and there's no foliage on the trees ... but even in summer when there's crops and leaves to absorb the sound, you can still hear them. Well, I can, but I have good hearing. I've always been able to hear things others couldn't hear … but most folks in these cottages can hear the bells at Tusham if there is nothing else to drown out the sound.'

'So, midnight?'

'Yes.'

'Hear anything else?' Ventnor asked.

'Any names?' suggested Webster.

'Well, if you can call them names, Animal and Soldier and the girl was not happy … she was crying … sobbing … she was upset alright.'

'Animal and Soldier?' Ventnor smiled. 'Plus a lass.'

'Yes. Does that help you?'

'Enormously.' Ventnor continued to smile.

'Then two bikes left … it was morning before the third bike left. I heard it … didn't see it, so I stayed in my bed. Thursday is my day off, so I was enjoying a long lie-in. Then I saw the smoke, so I got up and the house was well alight. I saw Mr Langley, who lives along the road from the house, I saw him dash into his house … he has a phone, so I thought he was phoning the fire engine and I thought right because they arrived, three of them, from York, but by the time they got here, the house was burned up. The flames were already beginning to die down. So, is it true they found a body? That man? The one who's been living there for the last few years ... him ... keeps himself to himself? Is it true?'

'Possibly.'

'I'd say probably,' Miss Oxterby said with a smile, 'otherwise you wouldn't be knocking on old Katie Oxterby's door, would you?'

'Well, we can't say yea or nay ... but you might be right.' Webster glanced around him. 'You'll have to wait until you hear it on the news.'

'No phone, no radio, no TV ... nothing like that. I cycle into the village once a week to get me provisions. I don't eat much because I eat at the farm ... three meals a day ... so it's not a bad job I got. Anyway, once a week I buy a newspaper to see what's going on in the world, and once a week I get the talk about what's going on in these fields and cottages. Reckon all the talk will be about the fire, come Saturday ... I'll hear it all then.'

★ ★ ★

The University Arms was quiet. One middle-aged man stood at the bar, sipping a pint very slowly, his mind more occupied with the contents of that day's *Yorkshire Post* than it was with the beer. The bar staff busied themselves cleaning and polishing, looking busy as their conditions of employment dictated. Away from the bar in one corner, two silver-haired ladies sat together in complete silence, each in front of a schooner of sherry, and each seemingly reluctant to drink their drink, as if the sooner they started to drink, the sooner they would finish and the sooner they would have to return home. The only other two people in the lounge, two men, were sitting in the opposite corner to the two ladies. They sat side by side, each holding a pint of beer.

'But you've got children,' one of the men said to the other as he swilled the beer around in his glass. 'Something to live for. Someone ... something to come out to ... me, I am free of that.'

'You have your fiancée...' the other replied.

The first man cast him a pained glance. 'How long do you think she'll be my fiancée for when she hears about this? You see, I am free to do it ... it makes sense. What do you think we'll get? Ten years, I'd say.'

The other nodded. 'Minimum.'

'You see ... where will that leave us? Mid-fifties ... no employment prospects, life on the dole. It's a long way for us to fall. Do you want to fall that far?'

'Nope.' The man sipped his beer, then placed it on the table. 'Damned stuff tastes sour all of a sudden.'

The other man forced a smile. 'I'd make the most of it if I were you ... neither of us will be getting much of that in the next ten years ... and as you say, that's minimum!'

'I'm going to lose everything ... everything.'

'Me too.'

'My licence ... can't have one with a criminal record ... especially for murder.'

'Very especially for double murder ... very, very especially. Can't do my job either.'

'My wife will divorce me. Oh God, I still have nightmares about it.'

'Me too.'

'There's a lot more to consider than gaol time if you commit a crime. Why? Why did we get into it?'

The first man shrugged. 'Seemed a good idea at the time.'

'Seems like it all belongs to a different life-time.'

'Doesn't it?' The first man paused. 'Have you noticed how much more immediate life is? How colours are louder? How smells are stronger? How you can find beauty in a blade of grass?'

'So, you are going to do it?'

'I think so ... I can't fall from this height. Feigned illness to come and talk to you. That's not far from the truth.'

'I can understand ... I still might do the same but my children need a father ... even if he is a divorced gaol rat with no prospects at all upon release.'

'I know. It's alright for the others, this will be like a feather in their caps.'

'Hawson will be afraid ... but not the others.'

'Supposing we get their first? To the cops, I mean? Like he said, start to help our-selves?'

'You can if you like. We'll get less time in the slammer but five years ... ten years, it doesn't matter. That's not the price you and I have to worry about, but you go your way, I'll go mine. It's only my children stopping me going with you ... and I might still ... don't know.'

Hennessey strolled off Navigation Road and into Speculation Street and then into the Old Speculation Pub being, he had found, fondly and jealously guarded by the locals, not wanting its presence known to the tourists or to university students. It was their pub, and that's how they wanted it kept and the publican too was happy with things just the way they were. A nice, quiet pub kept financially viable with the same few customers who wanted simple, homely drinks rather than trendy cocktails, manufactured for the youth market.

It was quiet too in the Speculation, no music, no television screens with the sound and the contrast turned up too loud. Just a lovely, lovely pub which had not, to Hennessey's interested but admittedly untrained eye, changed a great deal from when it was built in the closing years of the reign of Queen Victoria. Inside, the ceilings of ornamental plaster were lower than usual, even for York. There were polished wood panelling, solid wooden chairs in front of solid wooden two-tiered tables, so designed to accommodate drinks on the lower tier whilst the top of the table could be given over to cribbage or dominoes. Horse brasses hung on the wall; a collection of shell casings from World War I occupied a shelf above the fireplace. A dartboard was presently soaking in a pail of water beneath its rightful hanging place, which would be taken out and placed, dripping, on the wall at approximately six p.m. in anticipation of the evening trade.

Shored-Up, sitting at a corner table, smiled as Hennessey entered the snug. Hennessey nodded in recognition and walked to the small bar and pressed the brass bell, sending a metallic 'ping' around the silence of the pub. When a young barmaid, pleasingly, he thought, with a local accent, responded, he ordered the drinks: a whisky and ginger for Shored-Up and a soda water and lime for himself.

'Need your help, Shored-Up.' Hennessey sat on the chair opposite the man and placed the whisky in front of him.

'And I need yours, Mr Hennessey. I am going to be breached by my probation officer. Delightful girl, just doing her job, but I really do not want to return to within the gates.'

'What have you been up to?'

'Oh, nothing, Mr Hennessey, nothing. It's rather what I haven't done...'

'Not been keeping your appointments?'

'Missed the last three, Mr Hennessey.' Shored-Up sipped his drink. 'Nectar ... nectar.'

'Three? That probably means four or five.'

'Well, it's always better to understate ... but she does give me such awful times ... ten a.m ... .just as I usually rise. To get to a ten a.m. appointment, I'd have to rise at 8.30...'

'Well, try telling that to all those old ladies you have fleeced out of their life savings...'

'Hardly life savings,' he said with a smile.

He was a small, slightly built man who wore a lightweight Italian cut overcoat, a gold watch, a panama, cavalry twill jacket, highly polished brown shoes and did indeed, Hennessey conceded, manage to cut quite a dash despite all the clothing and the watch being purchased from charity shops. It was necessary to enable him to pass himself off as Lieutenant Colonel Smythe (Retired) of the Devon and Dorset Regiment. He had, he once explained to Hennessey, passed himself off as a retired officer of the Green Howards, but that, being a Yorkshire regiment, there was, he felt, too much danger of running into the real thing. Consequently he had decided to use the name of a West Country regiment to impress aged gentlefolk who had money to invest in Bolivian tin mines or the salvage operation of a treasure laden Spanish galleon. 'Only what my clients could afford to spend.'

'Or lose.' Hennessey smiled. 'And clients is hardly the word.'

'Ah...' He shrugged. 'I do always emphasize that there is an element of risk.'

'There you're wrong, Shored-Up, with you there is no risk at all; there is total certainty that you'll take their money and that's the last they'll see of it or you. You know, one day you are going to talk about your victims and when that happens I will know the probation officer is getting somewhere ... if you should deign to keep your appointments.'

'So could you help me, Mr Hennessey? Prison food and those clothes they make you wear ... and those rough boys.' Shored-Up shuddered.

'Well, I'll see what I can do. I'll probably only be able to get her to give you one more chance, but if you go on failing to keep the appointments ... well, it's the big house for you ... again.'

'Oh...'

'Donald Pickworth.'

'Ah...'

'That name means something to you. I saw that look in your eyes.'

'You are looking for Don?'

'Yes. Do you know him?'

Shored-Up drained his glass and, putting it on the table, pushed it towards Hennessey. 'I know *of* a Donald Pickworth.'

'So do we, we have previous, but he has disappeared ... not at the last address.'

'Sounds like a dip artist ... Pickworth.' Shored-Up laughed at his own joke. 'Get it?

Pickworth?'

'This Pickworth was a big name, a serious player in the York area ... had a heroin distribution network.'

'Cocaine.'

'Sorry?'

'It was cocaine ... He probably did heroin as well, but I remember him for distributing cocaine. This was about twenty years ago now? Pickworth ... dip artist ... perfect name for a dipper.'

'Yes ... must be the same Pickworth.' Hennessey remained stone-faced.

'Has to be.'

'Where do we find him?'

'Wharfedale House,' Shored-Up smiled.

'Wharfedale House! The Salvation Army hostel?'

'The very same. How the mighty fall.'

It was Thursday the twentieth of June, 17.47 hours.

Eight

Friday 21 June, 09.30 hours – 20.30 hours.
Also Wednesday, 24 December, 16.30 hours
– 17.30 hours
in which our tale concludes.

'We could go now...' Yellich suggested. 'Round 'em all up, Bannister, Anglis, Strubby, Heath, Zielinski. Bannister and Anglis are ready to crack. We have Miss Oxterby's evidence hearing Animal's name being used.'

'Soldier, too.' Ventnor sipped his tea.

'Yes, it's all there, boss.' Yellich appealed to Hennessey. 'We'll lean on Bannister and Anglis for the murder of Amanda Fryston and the other three for the murder of Harry Turner.

Hennessey stroked his chin. 'You say that Mrs ... or Miss Oxterby made reference to a

271

female ... she heard a female's voice at the time that Harry Turner's house was invaded?'

'Yes, sir.' Webster replied sharply, attentively.

'And that this female was distressed?'

'So she said ... she sounded to be distressed.'

'Find her.' Hennessey glanced at Webster, then Ventnor.

'Sir?'

'Find that woman. If she was as distressed as Miss Oxterby says, she'll be the one we need to speak to. She's our "in". She'll be the partner of Strubby or Heath or Zielinski.'

'Won't be Zielinski. We've visited him, he's got children,' Ventnor mused aloud. 'My guess is that one of the other two has got himself a younger girlfriend. We need to call on Heath or Strubby.'

'OK.' Hennessey nodded. 'You two do that. Yellich...'

'Skipper?'

'You and I are going to visit the Salvation Army.'

'The Sally Army?'

'Yes.' Hennessey stood and reached for his panama. 'I'll tell you on the way.'

'Don't know his story, really.' Captain Lavine was a slender, fresh-faced woman in her thirties, guessed Hennessey. He found her genuine and eager to please. She stood behind a reception counter in the disinfectant-smelling foyer of Wharfedale House. 'He was here when my husband and I took over from the last army officers.'

Hennessey was about to query the identity of the army officers when he suddenly realized that the reference was not to the soldiers but officials of the Salvation Army. 'The Stewarts ... they retired after over thirty years' service, much of it in India. The Army brings overseas officers home towards the end of their service life.'

'I see.' Hennessey smiled.

'You start out at home and finish at home but you can refuse a posting without having to leave the Army,' she said with a smile. 'My husband and I have decided to go wherever we are sent, and whenever, but Donald ... he's in the television lounge. Excuse me ... Nigel,' she called. 'Nigel?' She smiled at Hennessey. 'He's just joined the Army but he's very keen. Ah ... Nigel.'

Nigel was a short, thin young man with a pointed nose, weak chin, and who wore thick-lensed, black-framed spectacles. He was, thought Hennessey, the sort of loner who has 'target' written all over him. He approached Hennessey nervously.

'Nigel, will you please take these two gentlemen to the television lounge? They want to speak to Donald.'

'Donald?'

'The resident with the crutches.'

'Oh, yes...' Nigel turned and walked unsteadily away.

'If you'll follow him,' said a grinning Captain Lavine. 'He doesn't say much but he's a good boy.'

Nigel walked from the foyer into a large room where plastic-covered armchairs were arranged densely on the floor area, occupied by men who seemed to sit and stare at the huge television screen, which was mounted on the wall beside and above the door. Some of the men were painfully, tragically young, Hennessey noted, though most were in their middle years or older. He turned and glanced behind him and saw that the television was utterly incongruously showing a children's programme, but no one seemed concerned. It was a television and it was switched on and just as the Lavines would go when and where they were sent, the residents would watch whatever was on television whenever it was on. Nigel walked up to a middle-aged man who sat cradling two aluminium crutches. He had a patch over one eye and was in need of a shave. Nigel stood by the man for a few seconds and then walked away. Hennessey and Yellich glanced at each other, the good boy really, clearly, didn't say much at all, as Captain Levine had promised.

'Mr Donald Pickworth?'

'Aye,' the man growled, 'that's me. You look like lawmen.'

'We are.' Hennessey showed his ID.

'Long time since the law's been interested in me.'

'Mind if we join you?'

'If you like ... I could use the company.'

Hennessey sat in the brown chair to Pickworth's right, Yellich the orange-coloured chair to Pickworth's left.

'What happened?' Hennessey pointed to the crutches.

'I got rolled. These are my only friends now ... my two sticks.'

'Who by?'

'Don't know ... know who had it done, but I can't tell you. If I grass, I'm dead. I was in the business. I was in a good way of business.'

'Yes ... supplying cocaine and heroin.'

Pickworth rolled his eye towards Hennessey. 'I'm not admitting to anything. Don't you think this is prison enough? Look around you ... I'm here till I die ... and in this body ... two prisons.'

'Well, it was twenty years ago ... and without a confession we probably couldn't produce enough evidence to charge you.'

'So, what do you want?'

'Help ... we want your help.'

Pickworth forced a smile. 'Me help the law? I don't think so.'

'Remember a guy called Hawson ... Richard Hawson?'

Pickworth looked down. 'Him! Do *I* remember *him*?'

'I see you do.'

'He was the beginning of my bad luck.'

'Yes ... so we gather ... his courier service lost a brick of heroin.'

'Aye ... I had a Jaguar and a big house in the Vale ... had a name on the gate Sunny Deane ... like posh folk. It was going great for me, then it fell apart. After that brick went missing my name was no good. You got to keep your end up in business. I lost my contacts ... all moved on by now. I was back to small-time crookin' ... had to sell my house. I existed but was never up before anything more than the magistrates ... no Crown Court for me. So, no respect for me any more ... I had a Jaguar once and a big house in the Vale ... then this happened.' He tapped his two crutches together. 'I got the blame for a bit of money that went missing ... a few thousand pounds ... but I never, it wasn't me, but I got the blame. I mean, do you think I'd be stupid enough to hang round York if I had put my hands in the big man's pot? But it's not like the law ... you don't need proof. In crookin' you just need suspicion. So I got rolled ... I was made an example of, tried to blind me and put me in a wheelchair but the docs saved one eye and after six months the hospital got me to be able to hobble. They didn't come back; they must have been satisfied with how they left me. Nice of them, don't you think?'

'We're looking to nail Richard Hawson,' Hennessey said softly.

'What for?'

'The murder of Mandy Fryston and her boyfriend Terry North. It was Mandy Fryston that stole the brick. She got her boyfriend mixed up in it ... they were both murdered.'

'Someone went down for that.'

'Aye ... wrongful conviction, so we want the right guys.'

'So, what do you know?' Yellich asked.

'I can't tell you without implicating myself.'

'Well, let's keep it off the record, shall we? No tape-recorded interviews, no written statements. I mean, Hawson must have wanted to get back in your favour.'

Pickworth nodded to Yellich. 'He'll be a witness.'

Hennessey looked at Yellich. 'Would you mind, sergeant?'

'Not at all.' Yellich smiled as he stood and

walked back towards Captain Lavine and the reception area.

'So...' Hennessey settled back into the chair. 'You know the police will not prosecute unless there is a purpose to be served and, as you say, you are already in a form of prison ... two forms, as you said yourself. The crime was over twenty years ago, serious as it was ... but to prosecute you now, in your condition, would be repressive and, if you give information which leads to the conviction for murder, you are pretty well guaranteed to escape prosecution.'

'Pretty well? Only pretty well?'

'Yes. Unless you had a hand in a murder, the Crown Prosecution Service won't turn a blind eye to that.' Hennessey took out a packet of cigarettes and offered one to Pickworth who snatched at it greedily. Hennessey lit it for him with a disposable lighter.

'So, what can you tell me?'

Pickworth inhaled deeply. 'Not supposed to smoke in here...' Pickworth grinned at Hennessey. 'When that lad Nigel smells the smoke, he'll walk up and stare at me until I put it out and then he'll walk away ... never says a word, that lad.' Again he inhaled. 'Not joining me? Smokers like each other's company.'

'I'm not a smoker. I carry a packet of nails and a lighter because they come in useful.'

'Like now?'

'Like now.'

'I could use the rest of the packet if you don't smoke.'

'I could use some good information.'

Pickworth nodded. 'Alright ... nowt for nowt.' He inhaled and exhaled the smoke through his nose. 'Well ... Hawson hadn't got the control of his biker gang that he thought he had and when two of the gang burned me by stealing the brick, he needed his street cred back if he was going to go anywhere in this business.'

'We know that.'

'So, he had that boy and that girl cooled.'

'You have proof?'

'He told me he was going to have them cooled. He said we had both got burned. He had to pay me for the brick so I wasn't out of pocket, but I couldn't deliver the brick, so I lost my street cred. It was like he wanted to be on my side. "We've both been burned," he said. "I'll sort the pair of them."'

'He said that?'

'Yes.'

'Any witnesses to that?'

'Yes ... when I was a name I used to sit in the snug of the Golden Ball. You know the Ball? Down Hungate, off the Stonebow...'

'Can't say I know it,' Hennessey replied.

'You won't ... it was a real blaggers' den back then, a home from home for every villain in the Vale. Got a new licensee now ... straight guy, wants to make honest pennies and only honest pennies. Doesn't like any ducking and diving going on in his pub. But back then ... anyway, I had the snug two nights a week, Tuesday and Thursday, that's where I did business. So Hawson comes in like a hard man with his lieutenant, the one called Animal, and that's when he says he's going to have them chilled ... or cooled ... can't remember ... chilled or cooled but it means the same.'

'So, Animal heard him?'

'Yes.'

'We need an independent witness.'

'Well, all my boys were in the snug, they all heard him.'

'Got a name or two?' Hennessey asked. 'It

281

can't hurt them, they were not involved.'

'Let me think? It can't hurt them in this case but they've got their reputations, talking to lawmen could ruin them.'

'Understood.'

'Some of them are doing well. The clever ones are now people smuggling, just as much money to be made but the penalties are less. I mean, twenty years in gaol for smuggling cocaine, against four for people trafficking, for the same money.'

'I see.'

'Got to think of one who might grass. They'd want something for it.'

'We don't buy information.'

Pickworth drew on the cigarette. 'This is to nail Hawson?'

'Yes.'

'Well ... try Sid Bentham.'

'Where is he?'

'He's a tangy ... lives on the Tang Hall near the fortress. He was rising with me ... he was my lieutenant ... he fell with me and never did anything again. He's got no love for Hawson. Tell him I said to talk to him. He'll roll over.'

'That's something. Hoped for more, to be

frank, but it's something.'

'There is more.' Pickworth smiled. 'A few weeks later they came back ... Hawson and the guy they called Animal ... looked pleased. They said it had been done, both had been chilled. They left the lass where she'd be found, but the boy would never be found ... so he said.'

'This is better.'

'Then the boy Animal, he said, "We made the nancy boys do it. They didn't want to do it but they had to or we'd have killed them. They needed to prove they had bottle ... they did it, alright".'

'This is what I wanted to hear.'

'Then Animal said, "We fitted someone up for the girl ... he had it coming so don't worry about him". Hawson didn't look happy but he seemed to go along with it, like he felt he had no choice if he wanted to keep Animal on side.' Pickworth drew on the cigarette, taking it down to the butt, which he dropped on the floor and crushed beneath his shoe. Hennessey noticed his leg movement to be weak, uncoordinated, and apparently causing him considerable discomfort.

'You'll give a statement to that effect?'

Pickworth paused. Then he said, 'Yes ... yes, I will. Hawson did a lot of damage ... he needs to go down ... and go down for a long time.' He paused. 'I had a Jaguar once ... and a house called Sunny Deane.'

Hennessey handed Pickworth the packet of cigarettes and the disposable lighter. He joined Yellich, who was standing by the door. Close to him a resident of Wharfedale House was giving Nazi-style salutes to the passing traffic.

'How did it go, boss?' Yellich asked. 'You look pleased.'

'I am. Major crack ... major breakthrough.'

'What now?'

'We go to Tang Hall, we need to do a criminal record check, get the address of one Sid, that will be Sydney, Bentham of Tang Hall. We'll get that over the radio on the way there.'

The Pike and Heron pub stood in the centre of the Tang Hall estate. It was a square, brutal, brick building, surrounded by pitted asphalt and a low wall containing the asphalt. The pub was known locally as the Fortress. Hennessey and Yellich opened the door of the taproom and saw Sydney Bentham sitting alone in front of a half-drunk pint of beer. He was missing his left arm. The left sleeve of his jacket was doubled back and held in place at the shoulder by a safety pin. He held eye contact with Hennessey and Yellich as they entered the room. A few other drinkers were in the pub and all conversation halted as the officers entered, then slowly picked up again as they sat down with Sid Bentham, who was an angry looking man, thin-faced, in his fifties. They explained their reason for visiting.

'Pickworth sent you, you say?'

'He suggested ... he didn't send us anywhere.'

'Good enough ... it all fell apart for us when Hawson did what he did ... or those two did what they did, but they worked for Hawson. Pickworth struggled on, then was blamed for something. He reckons he was innocent but they tried to kill him anyway and chopped my arm off at the elbow. It was Pickworth they wanted, I was just there...'

'Wrong place at the wrong time?' Yellich said. 'It happens.'

'Yes, it happens.' He drained his glass.

'So, Pickworth has told us ... Hawson and Animal said what he said they did?'

'Yes ... and just how they said it. Is Pickworth giving a statement?'

'Yes.'

'Then I will as well. Time Hawson went away.'

'We don't pay for information –' Hennessey reached for his wallet – 'but this is worth a drink. Is it safe to give you money in here? They all know we are the law.'

'Aye...' Bentham nodded. 'I'm out of the game now ... and there's no heavy boys in here, just Tangys.'

'OK ... we appreciate it.' Hennessey put a twenty-pound note on the table. 'There'll be another one when we take the statement. We'll do that at your house in a day or two.'

Bentham snatched up the note with a swift, smooth and practised gesture. 'I'm home in the mornings. Here in the afternoons.'

'OK.' Hennessey and Yellich stood. 'We'll call one morning, possibly tomorrow, possibly next week ... more probably next week.'

She was tearful. She was shaking with fear. She had a bruised left eye. 'Can you help me? Can you help me? I didn't know they were going to do that.' She stood, leaning against the door of her house in Holgate, not the part of York known to tourists, but the part behind the railway station, blackened, small, terraced houses. 'They said they were going to call on a mate. I went on the back of Ranker's bike. Animal and Soldier carried the petrol on the back of their bikes ... got to the house out in the country ... kicked the door in and overpowered this guy ... chained him to a chair ... told him what they were going to do. I screamed and ran but Ranker slapped me and made me stay. Animal and Soldier left early but Ranker stayed ... made me stay with him. This guy was crying ... he knew he was going to die ... burned alive ... for hours, he knew. Then in the morning Ranker put the petrol everywhere ... on him, the guy, and all around the house ... then struck a match. It was horrible, horrible. Can you save me from them? They're not human...'

'Alright, pet.' Thompson Ventnor laid a comforting hand on her shoulder. 'You come with us ... you're safe now.'

'Where is he? Ranker...?' asked Webster.

'Gone to see Soldier. They agreed to meet back at Soldier's drum when it was done.'

'What about the house? I'm supposed to look after it.' She turned nervously and looked back inside the cluttered hallway. 'Ranker ... he...'

'You leave the house to us, pet.' Ventnor coaxed her out of the house. 'It's a crime scene, we like it just as it is and Ranker won't touch you ever again.'

The twin spools of the tape recorder spun slowly. The red recording light glowed softly.

'I am Detective Chief Inspector Hennessey, the time is 12.42 p.m. on Friday, 21st June, the place is Interview Suite Two, Micklegate Bar police station, York. I am now going to ask the other people in the room to identify themselves.'

'Sergeant Yellich.'

'Miles Quirke, solicitor, of Ellis, Burden, Woodland and Lake, of St Leonard's Place.'

'Andrew Anglis.'

'My client, Mr Anglis, has come of his

own free will and wishes to make a statement of confession. I would like that to be noted.'

'So noted.' Hennessey nodded. 'So, Mr Anglis, in your own words...'

'Yes...' Anglis leaned forward. 'Strange ... I had my speech all prepared and now ... now it's gone.'

'In your own time.'

'I talked it over with him, then I told my wife, then my father ... my wife told her father and all the advice was the same ... turn myself in'

'Yes...'

'I think you should go and arrest John Bannister ... for his own sake. He can't see any future for himself, you see...'

'I am on it, sir.' Yellich leapt up and left the interview room.

'DS Yellich left the room at 12.44 hours.' Hennessey paused. 'Since this is a confession, freely given and in the presence of Mr Anglis' legal representative, the interview can continue with just myself to represent the police. So, Mr Anglis...'

'Well ... the boy Terry North and his girlfriend, stole some heroin from Richard

Hawson, the Dungeon Master, so called...'

'And so Richard Hawson had them murdered to try to regain his street cred with Donald Pickworth, who was a big time crook in York and the Vale and who now isn't,' Hennessey continued.

'He isn't?'

'No ... he cuts quite a pathetic figure now. All this we know, Mr Anglis ... Tell us what we don't know. Who did the actual murder?'

'I did ... myself and Bannister. When we used to ride with the Dungeon Kings we got a lot of hostility from the likes of Animal, Ranker and Soldier, they didn't like us ... we were ... we were...' Anglis struggled for words.

'Posh?'

'Yes, in a word ... but Hawson seemed to like that, so he protected us. The rest of the gang were indifferent, but when the brick was stolen, Hawson had to throw something to the wolves to stop them from deserting, and the wolves said, me and Bannister had to show we were hard enough to be part of the gang. They wanted us to kill ... to murder Fryston and North, and the Dungeon Master, Richard Hawson, agreed.'

'Go on.'

'Fryston and North were lured to a remote place near Ripon. They thought their excuse that they'd lost the brick had been believed. I mean, who loses a brick of heroin? Anyway, they were told it was a gang meet ... but it turned out their excuse hadn't been believed by Hawson.'

'He was there?'

'Oh yes. So were a few others ... not all of them are alive now. Coffin Dodger for one ... and Hawson wanted his brick back. Mandy Fryston said she'd thrown it in the river ... so she was dead then ... Terry North thought he was safe because it had all been Mandy's idea.'

'So, what happened?'

'I banged her over the head with the spade I'd been given. Bannister did the same to her as well. Then we left her body where it would be found, because Animal had an issue with a gang member called Harry the Horse Turner. He wanted to implicate Turner in the murder.'

'Was Turner there?'

'No ... he had nothing to do with it. He was wrongfully convicted. But his conviction took the heat off Hawson and the rest of the gang. The police at the time thought they'd wrapped it up, especially as Turner admitted his guilt after he had been convicted. Why he did that I don't know.'

'To win an early parole before the system destroyed him,' Hennessey growled.

'Which is what we want for you,' Quirke said with a smile. 'Now, the important point ... you haven't finished your story.'

'Yes ... we were forced to do it.'

'Forced?'

'Well, Animal organized it well ... the crew were armed ... iron bars, pickaxe handles, that sort of thing. They said, "Show us you can do it, nancy boys ... show us you're hard ... or there'll be three bodies in this field, not one."'

'Animal said that? Zielinski?'

'Yes ... Zielinski ... he was in charge that night. Animal and the Dungeon Master ... they were both in charge, but me and Bannister did the business. Then, a couple of weeks later they made us do the same to Terry North. He had thought he'd got away with it, but that was just part of the plan, to make him feel secure and then do him too,'

Anglis recounted with a shudder.

'Ahh. I thought it would be something like that,' commented Hennessey.

Quirke smiled again and looked over at Anglis. 'You have taken your first step to an early parole.'

'Dare say you have,' Hennessey said with a sigh, 'just as Harry Turner did, but unlike Turner, you won't have to worry about Hawson, Zielinski and the rest when you come out. Lucky you, eh?'

John Bannister never did like his doctor. He was sure that the man had once been enthusiastic and caring and determined to make a mark on the Health Service, but by the time Bannister met him, he was approaching retirement as a sour and uninterested man. He never held eye contact with his patients, but would sit at his desk, pen in hand, which was kept poised over the prescription pad, and as each patient sat down, would growl, 'What's wrong with you?' It had long been Bannister's intention to change to another doctor, but enjoying robust health, the need to do so had never been pressing. He was, in the event, pleased he had not sought another doctor, for that day the man's lack of care for his patients suited him admirably.

That warm and dry Friday he had phoned his place of work, telling them he would not be coming in because he felt unwell and had then phoned for an appointment with his doctor. The man's unpopularity ensured that his was not a busy list and Bannister was able to secure an appointment for 11.10 that same forenoon. He had attended, and sat down in the chair in front of the man's desk and had said, 'I'm having difficulty sleeping...' and before he could complete the sentence, the prescription was scribbled, torn off the pad, and thrust into his hand. He had still not left the surgery before the doctor called, 'Next!'

Deciding to do it was the first step, and the second was deciding how it was to be done. Then he decided on the where of it. He had returned home and written a letter to his fiancée, brief and to the point, but he hoped sensitive, and wished her a good and full life, hoping that she would find happiness with someone else. He took a bottle of white wine from his refrigerator and walked to his car, dropping the letter in the postbox as he passed it. He drove to Whitby, parked his car and walked up to the abbey. There were a number of tourists visiting the abbey and the nearby church, which he knew had changed little since it was built, many, many years earlier. He walked across the adjacent field and hid from view behind a low stone wall, but from which vantage point he could look at the rooftops and the harbour and out to the North Sea. He plucked a blade of grass, and on examining it, found again the saying to be true: a blade of grass does have beauty.

Using his Swiss Army knife he took the cork from the wine bottle. He levered open the top of the plastic carton of pills and began to swallow them, six at a time, helping each mouthful down with a generous sip of Frascati.

That evening Gillian Stoneman sat at home, dressed, ready to go out and was puzzled why he was late. It wasn't at all like him, he was usually, nay always, always, always so punctual. She gazed at her ring and felt a warm, satisfying glow from within her chest.

Soon, very soon, she would be Gillian Bannister, wife of a chartered accountant who was soon to be a partner in his firm, and no longer a spinster counsellor in a hospice.

The trial of *Regina versus Hawson, Strubby, Heath and Zielinski,* who all entered not guilty pleas to all charges, was held at York Crown Court the following December. The trial was held over ten working days, concluding on Christmas Eve. The jury retired into conclave at two p.m. that day and returned three hours later, returned guilty verdicts in respect of all charges. The judge did not defer for reports but chose to move directly to sentencing. Andrew Anglis received a life sentence, but in recognition of his guilty plea, the information he gave to the police and evidence he had given for the Crown during the trial, the judge did not set a minimum tariff. Richard Hawson received three concurrent life sentences for conspiracy to murder Amanda Fryston, Terence North and Harold Turner, with a fifteen-year tariff which had to be served before parole could be considered. Norbert Strubby, Philip Heath and Stefan Zielinski similarly received two life sentences for conspiracy to murder Amanda Fryston and Terence North, also each with a fifteen-year tariff. Strubby, Heath and Zielinski further received life sentences for the murder of Harold Turner with a twenty-year tariff.

Having given their evidence, Webster and Hennessey returned to the court to observe the remainder of the trial. They studied the jury, trying to identify the person who stood out as the leader and who would be the foreperson, and occasionally glanced up at the steeply tiered public gallery. Among the public was a woman Webster recognized but couldn't place. She was dressed in black and seemed to be struggling to fight back tears. Only days after the trial did he realize that it was the woman who had started the investigation by reporting the confession of a dying man who was a patient in the hospice where she worked. He could not recall her name and wondered why she should be so distressed. She had, after all, by her public spiritedness, brought closure to the families of Amanda Fryston and Terence North.

Hennessey, Yellich, Ventnor and Webster stood in a circle on the pavement outside

York Crown Court at the conclusion of the trial. It was already dark; the east wind blew bitterly across the city.

'Their first major meal inside is going to be Christmas dinner,' Webster remarked. 'Auspicious or inauspicious, depending how you look at it.'

'Well, they dug themselves into a hole.' Yellich stamped his feet. 'Coming for a beer, boss? Time of year and all that.'

'Thanks, but no thanks ... I have other plans.' Hennessey walked away from the group and drove out of the brightly festooned city, out to Skelton, which he always found to be a delightful village, with its tenth-century church and ancient yew tree. He parked his car outside a black and white half-timbered house and crunched the gravel as he walked up the driveway to the front door. He pressed the doorbell.

The householder opened the door and smiled. 'The children were collected by their father this afternoon.' She hooked her finger under Hennessey's collar and pulled him over the threshold. 'We have this evening, tomorrow and Boxing Day, and Saturday and Sunday to ourselves.' She took his